The Case of
the Twisted Kitty

The Case of
the Twisted Kitty

John R. Erickson

Illustrations by Gerald L. Holmes

Viking

VIKING
Published by Penguin Group
Penguin Young Readers Group
345 Hudson Street, New York, New York 10014, U.S.A.
Penguin Books Ltd, 80 Strand, London WC2R ORL, England
Penguin Books Australia Ltd, 250 Camberwell Road,
Camberwell, Victoria 3124, Australia
Penguin Books Canada Ltd,
10 Alcorn Avenue, Toronto, Ontario, Canada M4V 3B2
Penguin Books (N.Z.) Ltd,
182-190 Wairau Road, Auckland 10, New Zealand

Published simultaneously by Viking and Puffin Books,
divisions of Penguin Young Readers Group, 2004

1 3 5 7 9 10 8 6 4 2

LIBRARY OF CONGRESS CATALOGING-IN-PUBLICATION DATA

Erickson, John R.
The case of the twisted kitty / by John R. Erickson ;
illustrations by Gerald L. Holmes.
p. cm — (Hank the cowdog ; 43)
Summary: After getting blamed when Sally May's car ends up in a snowdrift,
Hank suspects that this is another plot by Pete the Barncat to get him in trouble.
ISBN 0-670-03681-1 — ISBN 0-14-240041-6 (pbk.)
[1. Dogs—Fiction. 2. Cats—Fiction. 3. Ranch life—West (U.S.)—Fiction.
4. West (U.S.)—Fiction. 5. Humorous stories.] I. Homes, Gerald L., ill. II. Title.
PZ7.E72556Cat2004 [Fic]—dc22 2003058429

Printed in the United States of America

For a couple of new granddaughters:
Alyssa Erickson and ReAnna Wilson

CONTENTS

Drover's Violent Fantasies

It's me again, Hank the Cowdog. The mystery began in the depths of Panhandle winter, as I recall. Yes, January to be exact, the darkest, coldest month of the year. It was in the cold, dark month of January that I delivered Pete the Barncat his most crushing defeat . . . ever.

Remember Pete? He's your typical cat: arrogant, selfish, and not so smart. Keeping him humble and off balance is one of my most important jobs on this outfit, and I'm proud to report . . . well, you'll see.

I'll say only that the Cause of Justice was served. Pete got exactly what I deserved.

Where were we? Oh yes, January. In January, the ordinary routine of the Security Division is

1

interrupted by snow, howling winds, and frigid temperatures, as we dogs struggle just to get through the day. It isn't a month when we complete many investigations or invent new techniques for protecting our ranch. However...

You'll be amazed by this. Would you believe that during this particular January, I succeeded in inventing a revolutionary new technique for escorting vehicles off the ranch? It's true, and here's the very first news bulletin on how that happened.

Okay, let's back up a little bit and set the stage. A cold morning in January. Four inches of snow on the ground. Roads slippery and hazardous. All the trees and sagebrush were covered with a layer of frost.

Some dogs might have said it was a pretty winter scene. Not me. What's pretty when your gunnysack bed is frozen stiff? What's pretty when you have to tramp around in the snow, just to keep your gizzard from freezing solid?

That's what we were doing, Drover and I, the Elite Troops of the Security Division. We were tramping through ranch headquarters, trying to keep from being frozen into solid blocks of doggie protoplasm, following frozen dog trails that had been previously pressed into the snow by our feet.

As you might expect, Drover was moaning and

whining every step of the way. "Oh Hank, I'm so cold! I'm not sure I can walk another step. My paws are freezing."

"Then sit down in the snow and see how you like that."

"No, 'cause then my paws would feel better but my tail would be cold."

"I guess you'll have to choose: cold paws or cold tail."

"I'd rather choose between warm paws and warm tail."

"Fine, Drover. It's your life. Choose anything you want, but quit moaning and complaining."

"I think I'll choose . . . warm paws."

"Great."

We continued our march through headquarters. My paws were freezing, but did I moan and groan and make a spectacle of myself? No sir. When a guy has risen through the ranks and has taken over the job of Head of Ranch Security, he leaves the pampered life behind and learns to endure every sort of pain and discomfort. It goes with the job. We take the very worst that the weather can throw at us and . . .

Boy, my feet were frigid! I quickened my pace and tried to ignore the misery. It was then that I suddenly realized . . . Drover had stopped moaning and whining. I tossed a glance over my shoulder and was shocked to see that he was wearing a silly grin.

I halted the column. "Halt! Drover, we are conducting a march over frozen snow and brutal terrain, yet I notice that you're wearing a silly grin on your face. Would you care to explain yourself?"

His eyes came into focus. "Oh, hi. Were you talking to me?"

"Of course I was talking to you. To who or whom else would I be speaking?"

"Well . . ."

"Hurry up, I'm freezing. Answer the question."

"Well . . . I don't remember the question."

I searched for patience. "All right, one more time, and please pay attention."

"I'm all ears."

I narrowed my eyes and studied the little mutt. "What? You 'maul ears'? Is that what you just said?"

"No, I said, I'm all ears."

"Right. That's what I said you said."

"No, you said I *maul* ears, but I said I'm *all* ears."

"Exactly. And is it true?"

"Well . . . I guess so . . . sure. I'm all ears."

"Ah! There it is again." This was something new and puzzling. I began pacing, as I often do when my mind has been activated to a higher level of per-

formance. "Tell this court exactly what you mean when you say, 'I maul ears.' What types of ears are we talking about?"

"Well, let's see." He rolled his eyes around. "Just plain old ears. Dog ears."

"Aha! Dog ears. I'm beginning to see a pattern here."

"Yeah, 'cause ears hear. And we're dogs."

"Exactly. The clues are beginning to pile up." I stopped pacing and whirled around to face him. "Drover, has it occurred to you that mauling suggests brawling?"

"No, but they rhyme."

"They rhyme, but never mind."

"That rhymes too. Almost."

"Please stop talking about rhymes and listen carefully to my analysis of your problem."

"Gosh, I didn't know I had a problem."

"Of course you have problem, a very serious one." I marched over to him and looked deeply into his eyes. "Don't you get it? Mauling and brawling suggest an alarming shift toward aggressive behavior. Could it be that a little rebellious streak has suddenly burst out into the open?"

"Well . . ."

"Don't argue with me. Just look at the clues and follow the evidence. Yesterday, you were a happy little mutt. Today, you're talking about getting into fights and tearing the ears off your fellow dogs. What's happened, Drover? What has brought on this plunge into fantasies of violence?"

He stared at me for a moment, then grinned. "You know, I think you misunderstood what I said."

"Oh, so that's it. Now you're blaming me, huh? You're in the Nile, Drover, and you're in water over your head. For once in your life, face the truth."

"I said I was ALL EARS. That's all I said, honest."

"Huh? You said . . ." I marched a few steps away and tried to absorb this latest piece of news. "Let me get this straight. You said you were *all ears*?"

"Yep, that's what I said. I was ready to hear your question."

"You said nothing about brawling or fighting or tearing the ears off your fellow dogs?"

"Nope. You know me. I'm scared of fights."

"So . . . I might have . . . well, misunderstood your words?"

"I guess so."

I took a big gulp of air and let it hiss slowly out of my lungs. "So . . . this whole conversation has been more or less . . . pointless?"

"Looks that way to me."

I eased over to him and laid a paw on his shoulder. "Drover, I think it would be wise for us to keep

7

this conversation . . . well, a secret between the two of us. Don't you agree?"

"Well . . ."

"Good. I mean, we must do everything possible to protect the good name of the Security Division. If word ever leaked out that we were carrying on a loony conversation, it would do our cause no good. I'm sure you agree."

"Well . . ."

"Thanks, soldier. There just might be a little promotion in this."

"Oh goodie! A promotion! When?"

"Later. Now let's get out of here."

And with that, we re-formed our column and resumed our march through ranch headquarters, holding our heads and tails at proud angles. Once again, we had overcome the forces of . . .

I came to a sudden stop and turned to Drover. "Wait a second. You said you were 'all ears' and waiting to hear my question. What was the question?"

"Well . . . I don't remember, 'cause you didn't ask it."

"Hmmm. Good point." I furrowed my brow and probed the depths of my memory. Suddenly it came to me. "Ah, yes. We were marching along on frozen feet. I glanced back and saw that you were wearing a silly grin. The question is, Drover, when it's so cold

8

and miserable out here, why were you grinning?"

The silly grin returned. "Oh yeah. See, you said I had to choose between having cold feet and a cold tail, but I gave myself a third choice."

"This isn't making sense. Hurry up."

"I gave myself the choice of having warm feet, and that's the one I chose. Now I feel warm and happy. Are you proud of me?"

I gazed into the abyss of his eyes and found myself wondering . . . never mind. There's no future in wondering about Drover. He's . . . odd. Oh well. If he wanted to believe he had warm feet, if that brought a ray of happiness into his boring little life, that was fine with me.

We resumed our march through ranch headquarters. My feet had turned into blocks of ice but I didn't dare mention it or complain. Drover had ruined that option with his . . . never mind.

That's a weird little mutt.

We haven't come to the good part yet, my new technique for escorting vehicles out of ranch headquarters, but it's coming right up. Just be patient.

CHAPTER TWO

The Winter
Ski Patrol

W here were we? Oh yes, we were marching
through headquarters on frozen feet, except
Drover's feet weren't frozen. They were warm
because he had chosen to believe they were warm,
and that's pretty strange.

As we reached the southwest corner of the
machine shed, I cast a glance down toward the
house and noticed a very interesting detail. Sally
May's car was parked beside the yard gate and the
motor was running. It appeared that the car was
being warmed up, almost as though someone were
preparing to make some kind of trip or journey—
perhaps into town.

But why would Sally May be going to town on
such a cold and blustery day? This needed to be

checked out and I was just the dog for the job.

Have I mentioned that I'm Head of Ranch Security? I am, and very little happens on this ranch that I'm not aware of. If Sally May was thinking of driving into town on snack-poked roads . . . snow-packed roads, let us say, then I needed to check out the car and, you know, make sure everything was ready for the trip.

I gave the signal to turn our column in an easterly direction and we picked our way down the icy . . . PLOP. Oops, I slipped. We inched our way down the . . . PLOP . . . we made our way down the stupid hill which was a solid sheet of ice, don't you see, and the footing was very . . . PLOP . . . treacherous. No dog on earth could have made it down that icy slope without . . . PLOP . . .

Phooey. I stopped trying to walk and *skied* the last ten feet to the bottom of the slope. This was no big deal. Have we discussed our Winter Ski Patrol? Maybe not. See, the Security Division has its own Winter Ski Patrol and during periods of snowy weather, we activate WSP. And, well, I'm the leader. Maybe you're shocked that a ranch dog could have mastered all the skills required to glide down an icy slope, but let me remind you that . . . PLOP.

I made it to the bottom of the hill, is the point.

There, I picked myself up off the . . . that is, I turned my skis to the side and negotiated a perfect sliding plop . . . a perfect slopping stop, that is, while Drover skidded down the hill with no more grace than a cow on a frozen pond.

Once I had reached level ground, I marched straight over to Sally May's car and began making a thorough check of all the . . . HUH? A cat?

A smirking purring cat was sitting beside the yard gate. Would you care to guess who or whom it might have been? The main clue here is "smirking" and you've probably guessed Pete the Barncat. "Smirking" gives it away, doesn't it? It's one of the few things Pete does well. He never does any work on the place, but he seldom misses a chance to smirk.

And it drives me nuts.

I stopped in my tracks and beamed him a look we call "Nails and Broken Glass." The purpose of the N&BG is to throw a scare into the cat and melt that smirk off his mouth. It didn't work, so I lifted Tooth Shields and showed him two rows of sharp deadly fangs.

"Don't smirk at me, Kitty. I'm not in the mood for it."

"But Hankie, I wasn't smirking. I was just . . . smiling. Do you know why?"

A rumble began echoing in the caverns of my throat. "I don't know why, I don't care why, and I don't have time to waste talking to you."

He batted his eyes. "I watched you coming down the hill, Hankie, and it was . . ." He snorted a laugh. ". . . very entertaining."

Did I have time for this? No, but don't forget the Security Division's Shining Motto: *Do unto others but don't take trash off the cats.* It had become obvious that Pete was leading us toward a Trash Situation.

Would I back down? Ignore him? Walk away? No sir. The time to deal with a trash-talking cat is when he starts tracking tosh. Talking trash. Give 'em an inch and they'll take every nickel.

I swaggered over to him and stuck my nose in his face. "Do yourself a favor, Pete, and buzz off. Otherwise, I can't be held responsible for what happens."

He unfurled his long pink tongue and started licking himself on the left front paw. Right front paw. Who cares? He was licking a paw with his right front tongue, and I'm sure he knew how much it annoyed me.

"But Hankie, I'm just sitting here, minding my own business."

"Ha! Minding your own business? You expect

14

me to believe that? You were spying on us, Pete. You might as well come clean and admit it."

"Well, I did watch you . . ." He snickered. ". . . stumble and bumble down the hill."

"There, you see? You've proved my case. You were spying. If you had been minding your own business, you wouldn't have noticed that I . . . whatever you called it."

"Stumbled and bumbled down the hill."

"That's it. But for your information, Kitty, I didn't stungle and bungle. I was *skiing* down the slope."

"Oh really?"

"That's correct. If you're going to be a snoop, get the facts straight."

He stopped licking his paw and stared at me with his big yellow eyes. "I didn't notice any skis, Hankie. You came down the hill on your hiney."

"Of course I did. If you knew anything about winter sports, you'd know that Hiney Skiing is one of the most difficult of all skiing techniques. There aren't more than three or four dogs in the whole world who can do it right. Just ask Drover." I whirled around to my assistant. "Drover, tell this poor ignorant cat about Hiney Skiing."

Drover's gaze drifted down from the sky. "Oh, hi. Were you talking to me?"

"Will you please pay attention? Tell Pete about Hiney Skiing."

"Hiney Seeing? Well, if you want to see your hiney, you have to look behind you. I guess."

I gave him a ferocious glare. "Why do I bother trying to involve you in my business?"

"Well, you said . . ."

"Never mind, Drover. I'm sorry I asked." I whirled back to the cat. "Disregard everything Drover says." I whirled back to Drover. "This will go into my report."

"Gosh, did I do something wrong?"

"When we're conducting an interrogation of the cat, I expect you to stay alert and pay attention. You were staring off into space."

"No, I was looking at the clouds."

"All right, you were looking at the clouds. The point is that when I asked you to confirm what I said about Hiney Skiing, you failed to do it."

"Yeah, but I never heard of . . . Hiney Skiing." His eyes popped open. "Oh, you mean the way you came down the hill, on your . . ."

"Shhh."

Using one of the clever tricks we employ in the Security Business, I gave Drover three winks of my left eye. This alerted him that we were conducting secret business. Heh heh. Pretty shrewd, huh?

16

You bet. The cat didn't see it and never suspected a thing. Heh heh.

At last Drover grasped what was going on. "Oh yeah, Hiney Skiing."

I chuckled and gave the runt a pat on the shoulder. "You just forgot, right? But now you remember that Hiney Skiing is actually *a very difficult technique* that we've spent years perfecting, right? Explain that to Pete. He doesn't know anything about it."

Drover turned to the cat, who was watching us with a puzzled smirk on his mouth. "Oh yeah, we ski on our tails all the time. It's a very technical difficulty and we've spent many perfect years . . ." Drover turned to me. "What was the rest of it?"

"We've spent *many years perfecting it.*"

"Oh yeah." He turned back to the cat. "And we've spent perfect money protecting it."

I pushed Drover out of the way and marched back to the cat. "There, you see? There's eye-witness testimony from two of the Security Division's top executive officers. The next time you see us Hiney Skiing down a slope, I hope you'll show a little more respect."

Pete moved his eyes from one of us to the other, and he began twitching the last inch of his tail back and forth. "My goodness, Hankie, I had no idea. I thought you were just a couple of clumsy dogs staggering around on the ice."

Drover and I exchanged secret winks and grins. "Well, now you know, Kitty. It isn't every day that we can take time out of our busy schedules to improve your tiny mind, but this time we were glad to do it."

"Oh, thank you, Hankie! Thank you ever so much."

Heh heh. Can you believe it? The dumbbell ate it up, gulped it down, swallowed the whole thing. The truth is, it was nothing but a windy tale. Hee hee. No kidding. Hiney Skiing? Pure rubbish. I'd never heard of such a thing and neither had Drover, but we had used teamwork and superior intelligence to win another victory over the cat.

See, anytime we can pull nasty little tricks on Pete, we consider it time well spent. It's not only clean, wholesome entertainment for us dogs, but it also keeps the cat from knowing exactly what we're doing on the ranch.

That's pretty important. These cats need to be humbled on a fairly regular basis, don't you see, otherwise . . . well, they start getting wild ideas about who's in charge. Pete's even more inclined that way than most cats, and keeping him humble and off balance is a very important part of . . . we've already covered that.

Anyway, Drover and I had worked a perfect scam on Kitty-Kitty and . . . tee hee . . . I'm sorry, I don't mean to gloat, but our victory over the cat was delicious. We were very proud of ourselves. We were in the midst of a celebration of winks and grins when, all at once, the door of the house opened and out stepped . . . Our People.

Loper, Sally May, Little Alfred, and Baby Molly. They were the family who owned and lived on our ranch, the very ones we of the Security Divison had sworn a solemn oath to protect and defend.

As you might expect, my whole body began tingling with joy and excitement. Our People had come out of the house on a cold, miserable day, just to see and say hello to . . . well, ME, you might say, and maybe Drover too, but to a much lesser extent.

Our People had spent a long and lonely night inside an empty house . . . well, not exactly empty, but it was a house without dogs, and a house without a dog is like . . . something. It's a lonely place, just a cold, empty, echoing chamber. But now . . . they had come outside to see ME and to seek the kind of deep and meaningful companionship that only a dog can give.

Oh, happy day! I leaped to my feet and went

to Broad Swings on the tail section. Somehow, in the excitement of the moment, I stepped on the cat—Reeeeeer! Hisss!—and flogged him on the nose with my tail, heh heh, but that was no problem. I mean, when Our People appear on the scenery, my interest in cats drops to zero.

"Oops, sorry, Pete. Move out of the way and you won't get stepped on. You're dismissed. Good-bye."

Kitty crawled away, beaming me an icy glare. That was fine, he could glare all the ice he wanted and I didn't care. I had better things to do than worry about a shrimpy little cat.

Our People had come!

CHAPTER THREE

Pete and I
Become Friends

They were all bundled up in their winter coats and hats and gloves, even Baby Molly who was zipped up in some kind of thing that looked like a sleeping bag. A snow suit, maybe that was it, a pretty little pink snow suit, with a cap to match. And Sally May was wearing a furry hat.

As they came down the sidewalk . . . actually, you couldn't see the sidewalk because it was covered with snow . . . as they came down the invisible sidewalk, Loper said, "Hon, I'm not comfortable sending you off to town on these icy roads."

And Sally May said, "Oh, we'll be fine. I'll take it easy."

"If you could wait 'til I'm done feeding cattle, you could take the pickup."

"I'd rather go now and get it over with. The weather tomorrow might be worse. We'll be fine."

They came to the gate. I was waiting on the other side, trembling all over with excitement and antiperspirant. Anticipation, let us say. I was trembling all over with joy and longing. My heart was beating a wild rhythm in my chest. My tail whipped back and forth with such vigor, I could hardly keep from staggering around, I mean, we're talking about Broad Joyous Swings on the tail section.

My eyes were shining with dogly devotion. My ears were perked and my lips had formed themselves into a smile that said, "Here I am!"

I waited. I tried to be patient but, hey, this was tough.

Loper opened the gate for his wife. She stepped through the opening. Perfect! I went into Deep Crouch and sprang upward, throwing all my devotional so-forths right into the middle of her . . .

"Hank, get down!"

Huh? Okay, maybe I got carried away and threw a little too much devotion into the procedure, because she . . . well, the weight of my enormous body seemed to, uh, cause her to stumble backward, you might say, while I fell back into the snow.

But you know me. I'm no quitter. I picked

myself off the ground and went straight into the Reload Procedure. I recoiled my hind legs and prepared to ...

"Hank, for crying out loud, get away!" That was Loper's voice, and it sounded a little ... well, harsh, even angry. Oh, and he kicked snow at me. What was the meaning of ...

They all glared down at me—everyone but Little Alfred, that is, and he was laughing. Fine boy. But the rest of them ... yipes. Their eyes burned holes in me. My ears began to melt. My tail began to sag.

Sally May stepped forward and stuck her face right next to mine. "Don't jump up on me. I don't like that. No, no, no!"

Well, gee, I'd only been trying to ... I mean, they'd been inside the house all night without a loyal dog, and I just thought ... oh brother. Well, her face was right there in front of my nose and I was suddenly seized by the thought that, hey, the least I could do would be to give her a juicy lick on the face, right? So ...

SLURP.

"Stop that! Get *away* from me!"

Okay, I'd forgotten that she didn't appreciate, uh, Licks on the Face. I mean, we'd been through this on several occasions but in the heat of the moment, I had just ...

"Scat! Shoo!"

Fine. I could scat, but she didn't need to screech at me. Dogs have feelings too. In a flash, I drew my tail up into a position we call "Gee Whiz" and went slinking away. I slank over to the front of the car and took refuge behind the right front tire. There, I peeked out and listened to the rest of the conversation.

Sally May: "I wish you'd teach that dog some manners."

Loper: "Hon, he's just trying to be friendly."

Sally May: "I know he's trying, but he's . . . he's so *dumb*."

Boy, that hurt. You talk about an arrow piercing your heartmost heart! Her words pierced me deeply and opened such a huge wound, I wasn't sure I would ever . . .

"Gosh, Hankie, I'm sorry you got in trouble."

Did you hear that? Maybe not, since you weren't there, but I heard it. It was a familiar whiny voice, very much like the voice of a certain cat. I tore my gaze away from the scene at the gate, crawled out from under the car, and looked straight into the eyes of . . . Pete.

On instinct, my lips began to curl into a snarl. "You again? What did you say?"

"I said, I'm sorry you got in trouble with Sally May."

"Ha. Lies, Pete. You expect me to believe you're actually sorry?"

He gave me a look that seemed . . . well, almost sincere. I mean, he'd even stopped smirking. "I really mean it this time, Hankie. I saw it all. You were trying so hard to be a good dog."

"Well, yes, I was but . . . you really mean this,

Pete? This isn't one of your sneaky tricks?"

He raised his left paw in the air. "Honest, Hankie, Cat's Honor."

Well, this was almost too shocking for words. I mean, this cat and I had spent years building up a lousy relationship, and yet . . . I had to admit that he looked sincere. And he had mentioned a very crucial detail—that I was trying to be a good dog.

Well, at this dark moment in my history, I needed a friend, even if that friend was a cat. I heaved a sigh. "Thanks, Pete. As you can imagine, this is very discouraging."

"I know. Poor doggie."

"Right. I mean, sometimes I wonder what a dog's suppose to do to please these people. You wait for 'em to come outside and you spend hours preparing a little presentation to show 'em how much you care . . ."

Pete gave his head a sad shake. "And they don't appreciate anything. This is so sad, Hankie. I only wish . . . there was something I could do to help."

I stared at him for a long moment. "You mean that?"

He began purring. "Well, of course I do. We cats are very sensitive, you know. When we see others experiencing the pain of rejection, it makes us sad."

"Honest? I can't say I knew that and . . . okay,

maybe I've been overly suspicious, Pete, but you must admit that you've pulled some sneaky tricks on me in the past."

"I know, Hankie, and they were fun at the time, but now . . . well, what kind of cat would take advantage of a dog at a time like this?"

"Good point. Only a rat of a cat would do such a thing, and I mean a real genuine rat of a cat. And I guess you're saying that's not you, huh?"

He began rubbing on my front legs. "Oh no, Hankie, not at all."

"Hmmm, well . . . I must tell you that I'm shocked, Pete."

He looked up into my eyes. "You called me by my real name, instead of Kitty-Kitty."

"Yeah, well, if we're going to be friends, I guess it wouldn't hurt to . . . hey, Pete, I really appreciate your concern here, but I must tell you in all honesty that your rubbing gets on my nerves."

Get this. He stopped rubbing against my front legs! I mean, no growling or snarling, no argument, no fighting. He just . . . quit. And then he said, "I'm sorry, Hankie, I forgot."

I must admit that this blew me away. I mean, for years and years Pete had used that rubbing business to irritate me, but now he had quit—without a big scene. Could there be better proof that he had actually undergone a radical change, had decided to give up schemes and dirty tricks?

It was hard to believe all this, but the facts were beginning to overwhelm my ability to deny them. My misfortunes had touched Pete's heart, and he had become something we had never seen before: an honest, friendly cat.

Are you touched by the warmth of this scene? I was. It almost brought tears to my eyes but not quite. It was too cold for teary displays of emotion. Those tears will freeze on a cold day, you know, and who needs that? But as far as me being touched and moved by Pete's decision to become a Better Cat, an honest and sincere companion in a time of need . . . yes, I was moved and touched to the very depths of my inner bean.

At that very moment, as I searched for words to express my thoughts and emotions, I heard crunching footsteps in the snow. Sally May loaded the children in the backseat, closed the door, gave Loper a good-bye kiss, and trudged around the front of the car. When I heard her coming my way, I, uh, found myself creeping back beneath the car, so as to avoid . . .

I mean, let's face it. Only minutes before, I had been exposed to one of her Thermonuclear Moments, and I had every reason to think that she was still holding a grudge. She's bad about holding grudges, you know, and I had better things to do than to be on the receiving end of her scorching glares.

So I wiggled my way under the car and waited for her to walk around to the driver's side. Crunch, crunch. I saw her black snowboots pass by, and suddenly I realized that Pete was there beside me, under the car.

"You look surprised, Hankie."

"I'm shocked, Pete. I'm astounded. You could have walked Sally May around to the driver's side and gotten your usual pats and rubs for being a nice kitty."

"I know, Hankie, but . . ." He turned his eyes toward heaven . . . actually, toward the bottom of the car. Anyway, he lifted his gaze and heaved a sigh. "I just couldn't bear to leave you alone at such a sad time. I thought you needed someone to . . . share your sorrow."

Boy, what do you say to that? I was at a loss for words. Had this cat undergone a complete change of attitude or what?

The car door slammed shut and Pete said, "We'd better get you out from under here, Hankie, or you'll get squashed. Quick!"

"Hey, good thinking."

We scrambled out from under the car, just as Sally May put it in reverse and began backing out of the driveway. We watched her for a moment, then I turned my gaze on ... well, on my *friend*, might as well go ahead and use the word. It wasn't a word I had used to describe Pete very often.

"Thanks, pal. I got distracted, wasn't thinking. You did me a big favor there."

"Glad to do it, Hankie. I just wish ..." He heaved a heavy sigh. "I only wish I could think of a way to help you heal the wound with Sally May."

"I know, me too. But some wounds just don't heal."

"If only ... if only we could think of some heroic deed."

"Right, but it's too late for that, Pete. She's leaving the ranch."

We watched as Sally May gunned the motor, spun the tires, and started up the little hill in front of the house.

Suddenly Pete's eyes sprang open. "Wait! I've got it. You could run in front of her car."

"Huh? What would that do?"

"Well, you'd be escorting her, don't you see, showing your care and devotion."

"Yeah, but I still don't see ..."

"You could run very slowly ... to keep her from

slipping and sliding on the icy road. Don't forget, Loper was very concerned about that."

I ran all this information through Data Control. "You know, Pete, I think you've got something there. It would be heroic, wouldn't it?"

"Oh yes."

"And she'd be grateful, wouldn't she?"

"Oh yes, um-hmmm."

I placed a paw on his shoulder and looked deeply into his eyes, which seemed very sincere. "Great idea, pal. I think this will do the trick. Thanks a million."

I turned myself into the wind and went straight into the Launch All Dogs Program. As I roared away, I heard Pete's final words of encouragement. "Don't forget, stay right in front of the car . . . and *go slow*!"

"Got it, Pete! Thanks a bunch!"

And with that, I went streaking off to engage in Special Escort Duty.

CHAPTER FOUR

Special Escort Duty

Now you know about Special Escort Duty. Pretty impressive, huh? You bet. I mean, how many dogs would go to the trouble of providing such a valuable service to their misters and mattresses?

Masters and mattresses.

Masters and mistresses. How many dogs would . . . so forth? Not many, I can tell you that. Very few. Only one. Me.

And what makes it even more impressive is that I came up with the whole idea on my own. No kidding. One minute I was sitting there in the snow, trying to think of some heroic deed that would score me some points with the Lady of the House, and the next minute . . . bingo! There it was: a Special Escort Service that would provide Sally May and her children a safe journey out of ranch headquarters on the treacherous icy roads.

Awesome concept.

Maybe you thought it was Pete's idea. Ha ha. Not at all. See, your average cat has a tiny brain and is incapable of generating large, noble concepts. They're pretty good at performing certain simple tasks, such as purring, rubbing, licking their paws, and mooching scraps, but give 'em a big job that requires a broad sweeping intelligence and they just can't handle it.

So, yes, I had come up with this new concept entirely on my . . . okay, maybe Pete had mumbled something about it, but we can attribute that to Dumb Luck. It had been a shot in the dark, in other words. After years of loafing on the job and following a pampered life, Kitty-Kitty had come up with one shrimpy little idea, but don't forget who took that idea and turned it into a bold course of action.

Me.

We'll give Pete credit for coming up with a pretty good shrimpy little idea, but give me credit for putting it into action. In other words, Pete had absolutely nothing to do with the Special Escort Duty. I'm sure you'll agree with that.

Anyway, I left Pete and went streaking around the north side of the yard. At this point, my plan had taken shape and had fallen into two stages.

During Stage One, I would accelerate to an incredible speed, somewhere between Turbo Three and Turbo Four. (No dog can hit Turbo Five in snowy conditions.) This would lead me directly into Stage Two: intercepting Sally May's car as she passed in front of the house. Then, during Stage Three, I would assume the Escort Position and lead her toward the county road.

Did I say it was a two-stage plan? Let's correct that. It was a three-stage plan.

Okay, Stage One went off without a hitch. I roared around the north side of the house, bending trees and melting snow in the blast of my jet engines, and you'll be proud to know that my timing was nothing less than perfect. I reached the front of the house just in time to leap into the middle of the road and assume the Escort Formation.

Stages One and Two had been accomplished. I was now ready to enter the crucial Third Stage, the actual business of . . .

HONK!

. . . giving Sally May and her children an official escort over roads that were icy and dangerous. I began trotting down the middle of the road. As you can see, success in Stages One and Two would mean . . .

HONK! HONK!

...would mean nothing if...did you hear a horn honking? Maybe not. Where was I? Oh yes. Success in the so forth would mean nothing if I failed to complete the difficult maneuvers involved in Stage Three.

HONK! HONK!

And the Stage Three maneuvers were very difficult. Think about it. First, I had to trot down the middle of a road that was...

HONNNNNKKK!

... slick and treacherous and covered with slick, treacherous ice. Second, while trotting down the treacherous icy road, I had to perform very complex calculations that would produce the Safe Speed Ratio.

"Get out of the road!"

To arrive at the SSR, we measure the speed of the vehicle, multiply it times the Slickness Factor of the ice, divide that by the number of tires on the vehicle (four), and multiply all of that times the gravitational force of the moon.

Pretty amazing, huh? You bet. I mean, a lot of people think we dogs just blunder into things ...

"Idiot! Move!"

... and never give a thought to what we're doing, but that is far from the truth. Very often, we find ourselves solving massive equations of numbers that involve Heavy Duty Mathematics and ...

Huh?

She was speeding up ... Sally May, that is. She was speeding up and closing the gap between us. Not only that, but it even appeared that she was trying to ... well, pass me on the left side.

That was odd. See, the whole idea of this maneuver was to prevent her from driving too fast on the slick road. So what was the deal? Why was she trying to pass me on the left?

HONNNNKKKK!

And why was she blowing her horn? Okay, maybe she didn't understand the basic concept of the fundamental so forth, but don't forget that it was pretty derned complicated. Even I had trouble working out all the math on this deal.

But I couldn't allow her to speed up and pass me. That would have ruined everything, so I had no choice but to alter my course and shift my Escort Position several feet to the left, putting myself once again in the path of her . . .

"Get out of the way!"

. . . automobile. Maybe you think this was easy, but it wasn't. Far from it. See, in order to make the necessary corrections, I not only had to drift to the left and maintain the Safe Speed Ratio, but I had to do it while throwing glances over my shoulder. That was a toughie, one of the most difficult tasks of my whole career.

As you can imagine, it caused terrible cricks to form in the neckelary region of my neck. Did it hurt? You bet it did. Terrible pain, but I'm no quitter. I moved myself into the path of her . . .

"Okay, buddy!"

HUH?

My goodness, all of a sudden she stomped on

the gas, jerked the wheel to the right, and came roaring up the road. Yipes, unless I was badly mistaken, now she was trying to pass me on the right side of the road!

Sally May, wait! No! It's not safe! If you're not careful, you'll . . .

Crunch, thud. Uh-oh.

See? I had tried to warn her. I had done my very best to give her a safe escort all the way to the mailbox at the county road, but then she . . .

How can I say this without sounding too . . . uh . . . judgmental? Maybe she just never understood the basic purpose of the Special Escort Duty. Maybe she got impatient. Maybe we'll never know exactly what possessed her to jerk the wheel and go ripping over to the right side of the road, spraying snow on me with both rear tires.

We just don't know why she did it, but it led to a tragic situation. The car went into a skid, don't you see, and plunged into a snowdrift in the ditch. She spun her tires and tried to plow her way through the deep snow, but the car came to a stop.

She was stuck in the ditch.

Sigh.

Well, I had done my best. I had tried to warn her about the dangers of driving too fast on slick roads. I had used my very body as a bacon to lead her down the middle of the road, and yet . . .

A beacon. I had used my body as a beacon.

A great silence fell over the ranch. There wasn't a sound in the car. Gee, maybe they were injured and . . . well, you know me. When My People are in danger, I rally to the cause. *They needed a loyal dog to rescue them and pull them out of their snowbound car!*

I went plunging through the snow and raced to the scene of the accident. I was getting worried and worrieder. Maybe they were hurt. Maybe I would have to do Jaws of Life, tear off the door with my bare teeth and pull everyone out of the . . .

The door flew open and out stepped . . . yipes! I had supposed the woman who stepped out of the car would be Sally May, but then I wasn't so sure. I mean, this woman came boiling out the door and she . . . she didn't look much like the Sally May I had known for so many years.

Her face was bright red, an angry shade of red, and her eyes seemed to be glowing with some kind of . . . well, fire, you might say. And her nostrils were flared out, almost as though . . .

You know, I got the impression that she was mad about something, and we're talking about seriously mad . . . volcanically mad . . . dangerously mad. But what could have made her so . . .

Okay, it came to me in a flash. She was disgusted with herself for getting the car stuck in the snow. That made sense. I mean, I would be the last dog in the world to say a critical word about the Lady of the House, but let's be honest. If she had followed her Special Escort Service down the middle of the road, she would be on her way to town right now. Instead, she had gotten . . . well, careless, let us say, and now her car was stuck in the ditch.

And, yes, the poor lady was blaming herself. She was angry and frustrated, consumed with feelings of guilt, furious that she hadn't followed my lead.

Poor Sally May! Suddenly my heart went out to her. Would I just stand there while she punished herself and blamed herself and suffered the agonies of self-criticism? No sir. A lot of your ordinary dogs would have walked away and left her alone, but I've never been that kind of dog. This was one of those dark moments when a woman really needed a loyal dog to, you know, share her pain and guilt.

In a flash, I switched all circuits over to a little program we call "I'm Here To Help," and made my way through to the snow to her . . .

HUH?

She was slouching toward me like a . . . well, like some kind of monster woman with fangs and claws. And her eyes . . . gulp . . . there was something really strange about her eyes, and I mean, we're talking about flashes of lightning and volcanic eruptions.

I stopped in my tracks and studied her face more closely. The hair on the back of my neck stood up and my tail froze in the Neutral Position. Her upper lip curled, exposing . . . yipes, long sharp fangs.

And then her voice broke the terrible silence. She said, "Idiot dog! Look what you've done! If I ever get my hands on you . . ."

HUH?

Never mind the rest. Just skip it.

CHAPTER FIVE

Monster Woman Invades the Ranch

Don't expect me to reveal the rest of the story. It was much too terrifying for the little children. You know about me and the kids. I don't mind giving 'em a little thrill now and then, but I don't believe in exposing them to the really dark and scary parts of my work.

No kidding. The children probably think they can handle the scary stuff, but they just don't know.

What kinds of scary stuff are we talking about? Well, here's an example. Let's say that a dog is out on patrol and gets called to the scene of a routine traffic mishap—a lady has skidded on an icy road and her car has gotten stuck in the ditch.

No big deal, right? The dog goes to answer the call, help the lady in distress, the usual stuff that dogs are expected to do in times of trouble, only he doesn't find a normal lady in the car. What comes flying out of the car is an Enormous Monster Woman with flaming eyes and terrible claws and . . . and sharp fangs.

And you know what she does? With her terrible claws poised above her head and her vampire teeth dripping the blood of her last victim, *she chases the dog through the snow*!

See what I mean? That's the kind of terrifying scary stuff that I can't share with the kids. If they knew the truth about my job, the awful things I see in the course of an average day, it might cause them to have nightmares. And that's why we can't risk . . .

Wait a second, hold everything. Unless I'm badly mistaken, I just . . . okay, it slipped out. I didn't intend to reveal the rest of the story about Monster Woman, but somehow . . .

So now you know the Awful Truth that you weren't supposed to know. Maybe you think I'm making this up, that it never happened. Ha. I wish. No, it's true, every last word of it.

How did Monster Woman manage to steal Sally May's car without my knowing about it? Where did she come from? At this point in the investigation, we didn't have any answers. All we knew was that sometime between 9:03 in the morning and 9:12 in the morning, Sally May's car was stolen by a crazy woman who ran the car into a snow bank and then chased the Head of Ranch Security over two acres of frozen pasture land.

It was one of the scariest events in my whole career. Why, if she'd ever caught me, there's no telling what might have happened, but we had every reason to suppose that she might have EATEN a dog if she ever caught one.

You'll be glad to know that I managed to escape. How? Well, she stepped in a hole and fell down in the snow, and that gave me just enough time to highball it out of there. I hit Full Turbos and headed straight to the machine shed, didn't slow down or relax until I was hidden away in the dark-est, backest corner.

There, crouched beneath one of Sally May's reject-chairs, I waited and listened. I could hear the rumble of an angry voice in the distance, then . . . a deep throbbing silence.

Whew! Boy, that had been a close call. I slith-ered my way out from under the chair and crept over to the big sliding doors, which had been left open just wide enough for a dog to squirt himself through. I peered out the door and looked in all directions. I heard footsteps coming. I was about to dart back inside and take cover when I saw . . .

Whew! It was only Pete, not Monster Woman. I stepped outside on trembling legs and took a deep quivering gulp of fresh air. Pete came toward me, rubbing his way down the side of the shed.

"My goodness, Hankie, what happened?"

"Pete, you won't believe this." I told him the whole story, every last chilling detail. He listened with eyes that grew wider and more astonished by the second.

"Oh, mercy me. Monster Woman!" He gasped, placing a paw over his heart. "I'm amazed that you survived, Hankie."

"Yeah, well, it never hurts to be a great athlete and to be in top physical condition. But where did she come from, Pete? How did she manage to steal Sally May's car?"

Pete rolled his eyes around and curled his tail around his haunches. "Well, Hankie, I saw the whole thing."

"You did?"

"Mmm hmmm. We cats are very observant, you know."

"Okay, let's get on with the debriefing, and be brief. I need facts, details."

"Well, let me think. When you ran around the

north side of the house, Sally May was driving up the hill in front of the house."

"Yes, yes? Something happened in front of the house? Hurry, Pete, I'm beginning to see a pattern here."

"Well, when Sally May drove in front of the house, this . . . this huge woman-like creature swooped down from a tree and . . ."

"Whoa, stop right there." I began pacing, as I often do when my mind is chasing clues. "You said 'huge,' Pete. How huge?"

"Oh . . . seven feet tall, maybe eight feet tall."

"That checks out. Okay, you called her a 'woman-like creature.' Is it possible that this phantom you saw was actually . . . Monster Woman?"

Pete gasped. "You know, Hankie, I never would have thought of that, but . . . yes. Maybe that's who she was." He turned away from me and made a snorting noise. "Monster Woman."

I stopped pacing and studied the cat. "Were you just laughing about something?"

"Me? Laughing? Oh no, Hankie. I'm sure you'll agree that this is no . . . snort guff honk . . . laughing matter."

"It certainly isn't. On this ranch, the sudden appearance of monsters is serious business." I resumed my pacing. "It's all fitting together, Pete.

Don't you get it? Monster Woman was hiding in the tree. Sally May drove past the tree and Monster Woman swooped down and hijacked the car. That's how it happened. Pete, I've just blown this case wide open."

"Oh my. Hankie, I'm so impressed."

"It had me stumped there for a minute or two, but when you supplied the details about her jumping out of the tree . . . well, that pretty well wrapped things up." I marched over to him and gave him a pat on the back. "Thanks, Pete. You see what happens when we work together as a team?"

At that point, something strange came over the cat. He burst out with some kind of loud sputtering sound and darted away from me. At first I thought he was . . . well, laughing, but that made no sense. Why would he be laughing when our investigative team had just exposed a dangerous female monster on the ranch?

He wouldn't. I mean, Pete was no genius, but he wasn't dumb enough to laugh about *that*. All at once I was filled with concern. Maybe the little guy had choked or something. Back in the old days, when we were fighting like dogs and cats, I wouldn't have cared if he choked. In fact, I would have considered it a privilege to choke him myself, but now that he had helped me solve a difficult case . . . well, it was a different deal entirely.

I rushed after him. "Hey, Pete, what's the problem? You're not choking, are you?"

Again, he made that sputtering sound. "Not choking, Hankie. Tee hee! Just coughing."

"Oh, good. For a second there . . . but I never heard anyone make a coughing sound like 'tee hee.'"

"Cold air. It constricts the . . . tee hee . . . throat passages."

"Oh. Well, that makes sense. Maybe you'd better lie down. That's a nasty cough."

"Thanks, Hankie. Tee hee! I think I'll do that. Teeee heeeee!"

Pete staggered away, coughing and sputtering. "Get some sleep and drink plenty of liquor. Liquids. Oh, and be on the lookout for Monster Woman. She might be hanging around for a while. Don't let her bite you on the neck."

Pete went into another spasm of coughing and snorting and made his way down to the yard. The poor little guy! I only wished there was something I could do to ease his suffering, but . . . well, I wasn't a doctor.

Pretty sad, huh? You bet.

At that very moment, as I was feeling sadness and concern about Pete's illness, Drover came up beside me and sat down. "Gosh, what's wrong with him?"

"He's very ill, Drover. I think he might be coming down with distemper."

"You mean he's mad?"

"Mad? Why would you say that?"

"Well, you said something about his temper and I thought you made him mad."

I heaved a deep sigh. "Drover, please try to pay attention. I said distemper. Dis-temper. Distemper is like pneumonia in cats."

"Oh. Then why don't they just call it pneumonia?"

"I don't know. Maybe distemper is easier to spell than pneumonia. Did you realize that pneumonia starts with *p*?"

"Gosh, you mean they wet the bed?"

"What?"

"You said that when cats get pneumonia, they wet the bed."

I stared into the emptiness of his eyes. "I did not say that. I said, the word 'pneumonia' begins with the letter *p*."

"I'll be derned. So it's really 'pew-monia'?"

"No, it's really 'NEW-monia.' The *p* is silent."

"Yeah, it'll sneak up on you."

"Exactly. It's very confusing, and that's why we

call it *distemper* instead of pneumonia. But the point is that Pete is a very sick cat."

"I'll be derned. I thought he was laughing his head off."

"He was not laughing his head off, Drover. He was seized by a terrible fit of coughing."

"Then how come he was saying 'tee hee'?"

My eyeballs rolled up inside my head. "Because, Drover, distemper often produces a distinctive symptom called Tee Hee Coughing. You have your Hacking Coughs, your Crouping Coughs, and your Tee Hee Coughs, and the Tee Hee Coughs are the very worst kind."

"I'll be derned. I never knew coughing could be so complicated."

"Everything is complicated, Drover. If you spent more time paying attention and less time goofing off, you would know just how complicated this life can be."

"I'll be derned." He began scratching at his ear. "I thought maybe he was laughing 'cause you got in trouble with Sally May."

I beamed him a steely gaze. "There, you see? This is exactly what I've been talking about. Once again, you lost concentration and missed out on one of the most exciting cases of the year, The Invasion of Monster Woman."

He stopped scratching and stared at me. "Monster Woman! You mean . . . there's a monster on the ranch?"

"Exactly. She attacked me in daily broadlight and tried to bite me on the neck with her bloody fangs."

Drover's eyes grew as wide as plates and be began backing away. "Oh my gosh, I think I'll go hide under my bed."

I found myself . . . uh . . . casting glances over both shoulders. "Not a bad idea, son. In fact, I might even join you. Let's get out of here."

And with that, we went streaking down to the Security Division's Vast Office Complex under the gas tanks, rode the elevator up to the twelfth floor, burst into our bedroom-office, and dived beneath our respective gunnysack beds.

Only then could we be sure that we were safe.

CHAPTER SIX

We Are the Victims of Treachery

Pretty scary story, huh? You bet. But don't forget that I tried to warn you.

Where were we? Oh yes, Drover and I had just hotfooted it back to our bedroom-office under the gas tanks, for reasons which should be obvious by now. Monster Woman was running loose on our ranch and nobody was safe.

Once inside the office, we took the only sensible course of action available to us—we dived beneath our gunnysack beds and went into Bunker Position. There, safe inside our armored bunkers, we waited and listened. Nothing. Not a sound.

No, wait! There was a sound . . . a clacking noise. At first I couldn't identify the source, but after running it through our Sound Analyzer . . . well, I still couldn't identify the source. In the silence of the bunker, I reached for the Microphone of My Mind and sent out an urgent coded message to the rest of the troops.

"Oatmeal, this is Sirloin. Can you read me, over?"

Silence. Then . . . Drover's voice came over the crackle of the radio. "Are you talking to me?"

"Of course I'm talking to you. This is the Security Division's special frequency. Who else would be listening?"

"Well . . . I don't know."

"Do you read me?"

"I don't think so. It's too dark in here."

"Drover, can you *hear* me?"

"Am I Drover or Oatmeal?"

"You're Oatmeal . . . unless you want Monster Woman to know your name, rank, and serial number."

"Oh. I get it now. Oatmeal's a cereal."

"Roger on that."

"But how come I have to be Oatmeal and you get to be Sirloin? It doesn't seem fair."

I let out a groan. "Oatmeal, forget about food and pay close attention. Over here in Bunker One we picked up an odd clacking sound on Earatory Scanners."

"Yeah, I heard it too. Over here. Over."

"An odor? You're picking up some kind of scent? Quick, give me a description."

"Well . . . I can smell a gunnysack odor, over."

I lifted my nose ten degrees and tested the air. "Hmmm. We're picking it up over here too. I wonder if it might be . . . wait! Hold everything. Oatbran, what we're picking up is the smell of our gunnysacks, so disregard all references to gunnysack odors, over."

"Yeah, *mine stinks.*"

"What? You've discovered a land mine? Why wasn't I informed of this sooner!"

"No, I said *mine stinks.*"

"Roger on that, Bran Flakes. The clues are beginning to fall in place: the odd clacking sound, the strange odor, and now you've traced it to a land mine in your bunker. At this point we don't know why the land mine has a bad smell or who planted it here in the office, but the important thing is, don't touch it! Those land mines are extremely dangerous. In fact . . . Buckwheat, this is T-Bone. Evacuate the bunkers! Repeat: evacuate all bunkers!"

I tripped the Emergency Alarm, went flying up six flights of stairs, and emerged into the light of daylight of day. Whew! That was close. Moments later, Drover came scrambling out of his bunker.

I looked him over. He appeared to be uninjured. "How are you doing, soldier?"

"Well . . . I'm all confused. I don't understand . . ."

"Never mind, we don't have time to discuss it. We've had a serious breach of security. Let's go straight into Alert Stage One. Ready? Go!"

Have we discussed our Alert Procedures? Maybe not, and there's a reason for that. Most of this stuff is so secret and highly classified, we can't discuss it with the general public, but maybe it wouldn't hurt to reveal a few details—if you'll promise not to blab it around. Promise?

Okay, Alert Stage One is our highest stage of readiness. In this stage of the procedure, two dogs stand back-to-back, looking in opposite directions. One dog surveys the North and West Quadrants, while the other conducts Visual Sweeps of the South and East Quadrants. That way, two dogs can spot enemy troop movements in all four directions.

It sounds pretty complicated, doesn't it? Well, it is complicated, but what else would you expect from the Elite Troops of the Security Division? Protecting this ranch is no ball of wax and sometimes it gets pretty derned complicated.

We went into the Stage One Alert Formation and did Visual Scans of . . . well, just about every-

thing. The seconds crept by and there were no reports of enemy spies or troop movements. But then . . .

"Drover, I don't want to alarm you, but once again I'm picking up that odd clacking sound. Can you hear it over there?"

"Let's see. Oh yeah, I hear it now."

"Okay, let's study the sound and try to identify its source. It could lead us straight to the person or persons who've been planting all these land mines."

"Well, I think . . . it was me."

"What? You planted mines in your own bunker?"

"No, the clacking noise. I was cold and my teeth were chattering."

"Your teeth were . . . but what about the land mine? You *did* see a land mind, didn't you?"

"Nope, not me. It was so dark in there, I couldn't see anything."

"So you're saying . . ."

The air hissed out of my lungs and the upper half of my body sagged. I marched a few steps away and looked up at the sky. A few flakes of snow were beginning to fall from the dreary gray clouds. Was that a clue? No.

I marched back over to my . . . whatever he was. "Drover, I must speak frankly to someone. I'd rather not share my deepest thoughts with a nincompoop, but, well, you're the only one here."

"Gosh, thanks."

"No problem. Drover, sometimes I feel that I'm being crushed by the awesome responsibilities of running this ranch. I mean, the mysteries, the investigations, the endless details wear me down to the point where I feel . . ." I paused and glanced over both shoulders, just in case we were being watched. "Drover, sometimes I get the feeling that we're involved in things that are . . . really *stupid*."

Drover gasped. "Gosh, no fooling?"

"Yes. I know that shocks you, but we must face the facts. That conversation we held in our bunkers . . . Drover, it was all garbage. There was no enemy spy and no land mine."

"Well, I wondered about that."

"Yes, and you know what else?" I began pacing. "I can't even remember why we took refuge in our bunkers. Obviously, we were fleeing from something . . . but what?"

"Well, let me think here. I can't remember either."

"There, you see what I mean? The pressure is getting to both of us, Drover. We're doing all these odd things and we don't even know why. Maybe we need a vacation, a few days off. Maybe . . ."

Drover sat straight up. "Wait, I remember now! It was Monster Woman."

I stopped pacing and froze. "You're right. Holy smokes, Droker, into the bunkers! She's probably spying on us this very minute!"

We dived into our bunkers, screwed down the hatches, and waited in the throbbing silence for something to happen. Nothing happened. The seconds crawled by. Then . . . a peculiar thought began crawling through the ant den of my mind.

"Drover, can you hear me?"

"I thought I was Oatmeal."

"You were Buckwheat, but let's skip all that. I must ask you a very important question. Did you actually see Monster Woman?"

"Nope, not me. But Pete did."

"Yes, or so he claimed. And you know what else? It was Pete who suggested that I escort Sally May's car down the road. He emphasized that I should *go slow*. Remember that?"

"Well . . ."

"And Pete was laughing his little head off. Remember?"

"Yeah, but you said he was coughing."

"I said no such thing. Are you seeing the pattern here?"

"Not yet. I'm too cold."

"There's a pattern here, Drover, a very disturbing pattern. Now listen carefully. In five seconds, we will leave our respective bunkers and meet in the Conference Room. There, we will hold a secret high-level meeting of the Security Division's highest-ranking officers. Ready? Go!"

Exactly five seconds later, Drover and I gathered in the Conference Room. Before the meeting began, I did a complete security scan of the room, just to make sure we hadn't been bugged and penetrated by Outside Forces. Only then did I take my place at the front and begin the secret presentation.

"All right, men, I'll get right to the point. We have just learned that Operation Monster Woman was a complete farce."

Sitting on the front row, Drover let out a gasp. "Oh my gosh, you mean . . ."

"Yes, exactly. We've reviewed all the files and records from the case and it's now clear that there was no Monster Woman."

"Gosh, you mean . . ."

"Yes, Drover. We've been duped. That wasn't Monster Woman. It was Sally May. She was merely mad and looked like a monster."

Drover blinked his eyes and grinned. "You know, I was going to say that, but . . ."

"But you didn't. You kept silent and allowed the entire Security Division to be dragged down into a disgraceful scandal. Because of you, Pete has made us look like monkeys."

"Yeah, but I didn't do anything."

"That is exactly the point, Drover. You did nothing. You stood back and allowed your superior officer to make an idiot of himself. How does that make you feel?"

"Well, at least it wasn't me."

"What? Speak up."

"I said . . . I hope I can live with the guilt."

I marched over to him and laid a paw upon his shoulder. "I'm glad this hurts you, son. It should. You really let us down this time."

He sniffled. "I don't know what I did, but I'll try not to do it again."

"That's the spirit." I lifted my head to a proud angle and took a deep breath of air. "Now it's all behind us, Drover. What's done is done. But this was the straw that broke the camel's haystack."

He gave me a blank stare. "What does that mean?"

"It means . . . WAR! Pete has inflicted a terrible wound, but like the mythical Tucson, we will rise again from the ashes."

"Phoenix."

"What?"

"I think it was the mythical Phoenix. Tucson's in Arizona."

"So is Phoenix."

"Well . . . how about Flagstaff?"

"Close enough. Like the mythical Flagstaff, we will rise from the ashes and seek our revenge on Pete the Barncat."

And with that, the room erupted in a roar of applause and cheering. It had been one of the most inspiring speeches of my entire career. The Security Division had come back from the edge of the brink and we were now at war with Mister Kitty Cheater.

CHAPTER SEVEN

The Geothermal Procedure

W ere you able to follow all of that? Maybe not, because it came at a rapid pace and involved classified information from the very highest levels of the ranch's Security Division, so let me summarize with a Three Point Summary of the most impointant porks.

Points, that is. Impointant points.

Important points.

Point One: Certain members of our Elite Forces made the mistake of establishing friendly relations with our Number One Enemy, Pete the Barncat, and I guess it's obvious by now that one of the guilty parties was . . . well, ME, you might say. Okay, let's come clean on this. I made a really dumb mistake. In a moment of weakness, I trusted the cat.

Point Two: Admitting this really rips me. How could I have made such a bonehead mistake? I should have known better. Oh well.

Point Three: Once the little sneak had won my trust, he set a trap to get me in deep trouble with Sally May. How? He proposed the idea, the perfectly stupid idea, that I should run in front of her car at a slow rate of speed.

Point Two: It should have been obvious that this was a trap, a trick, and a set-up deal, and yet . . .

Point One: I fell for it anyway. Trying to be a good dog, trying my very hardest to win back the love and affection of Sally May, I led her down the road . . . at a slow rate of speed.

Point Two: That's why she was blowing her horn and screeching at me. Remember that? At the time it was happening, it didn't make any sense, but now . . . well, it seems pretty obvious, doesn't it? Boy, this really hurts.

Point Three: The rest is history. She got impatient, tried to pass me on the right side, and got herself stuck in the ditch. The angry woman who emerged from the car and chased me through the snow was SALLY MAY, not some . . .

Point Two: . . . phony Monster Woman. There was never a so-called Monster Woman on the ranch. That was pure garbage, another sneaky, underhanded trick, and Kitty Kitty thought I was, well, dumb enough to fall for it.

Point Three: Okay, I fell for it. That's why the little wretch was sputtering and gagging. You thought he was coughing, right? Ha. He was LAUGHING at my misfortunes! He'd set the whole thing up and I had . . . phooey.

That's the end of my Three Point Summary of the Tragic Events. It wasn't easy to boil it all down to three points but somehow I managed to pull it off. And now you know the Awful Truth.

This is very embarrassing. I mean, when a guy takes pride in his ability to outsmart enemy agents and spies, it comes as a terrible blow when he has to admit that he's been outwitted by a nitwit.

Wait, hold everything. *Admit-outwit-nitwit.* Do you see the pattern here? All three words end with the same two letters, *i* and *t*. Could this be some kind of clue that might blow the case . . .

I don't think so. Just skip it.

Where were we? Oh yes, I was performing a duty which I absolutely hated—admitting that Sally May's precious, scheming little shrimp of a cat had made a monkey out of me. But let me hasten to add that this bitter experience had made me a smarter dog, wiser dog, a dog who had been through the Fires of Life; a dog who had been burned and scorched but who had risen from the ashes like the mythical Tucson and had once again raised the Security Division's noble banner on the Flagstaff of . . . something.

The point is that Pete had taught me bitter lessons about Life Itself and had left me smarter, wiser, tougher, and more determined than ever to triumph in the never-ending battle of Good Dogs Versus Evil Cats. In other words, what we had here was another *huge moral victory* over the cat. No kidding.

Even so, things were looking a little grim. Not only was the day cold and gloomy, but my relationship with Sally May had suffered another terrible blow. Her car was stuck in the ditch and it appeared that her trip into town would have to be cancelled. Unless . . .

Was there something I could do to free her car from the snow bank? Somehow in all the confusion and so forth, I hadn't thought of that, but now . . .

Drover and I left the Conference Room. "Drover, I just thought of something."

"I'll be derned. I thought of something once, but then I forgot it."

"Please hush and pay attention." As we made our way toward the house, I told him my plan for freeing Sally May's car from the snow bank. "What do you think of that?"

"Well . . . you really think it might work?"

"Of course it'll work. It's all based on science, the application of geothermal energy."

"Gee. Oh."

"Exactly. Gee-oh-therm-al. It means the scientific use of natural reserves of warm water. Warm water melts snow, right? Snow melts away and frees car. Car is free, Sally May is happy again. We win Big Points."

"Yeah, but . . ."

"I'm not finished. We have vast reserves of warm water within our very bodies, Drover, and we're fixing to harness the forces of nature to help a lady in distress." In the distance, we could hear the whine of car tires, as Sally May tried to plow her way out of the snow bank. "There, you hear that? She's in distress and we can help."

"Yeah, but this old leg is starting to act up on me again. I'm not sure I could hike all the way to the car."

I gave the runt a withering glare. "Drover, I'm giving you the opportunity to win back Sally May's love and devotion."

"Yeah, but that's your deal."

"What?"

"I said . . . this old leg's really starting to throb. Oh, the pain! Oh, my leg!" He limped around in a circle and collapsed in the snow. "There it went, drat the luck!"

I glared down at him. "Drover, is your leg actually hurting or is this another attempt to weasel out of an assignment?"

"No, it's real this time. Honest. I guess you'd better go on without me. I just hope I can live with the guilt."

"Hmmm. Well, all right, if you're being sincere about this."

"Oh yeah, very sincere. I don't know when I've had so much pain and guilt."

"All right, soldier. I guess we'll have to leave you here and go on with the mission. Good luck. We'll see you on the other side."

Pretty sad, huh? You bet. I felt sorry for the little guy. I mean, what lousy luck that his leg had quit him just before an important mission. I could see the deep hurt and regret in his eyes, as he realized that he had missed his chance to perform heroic acts, but . . . well, some of us plunge on to new heights of bravery and some of us fall by the hayseed.

I had no choice but to leave Drover where he fell, twisting in pain and guilt. One of us had to mish on with the mushion . . . mush on with the mission, let us say, to free Sally May from the frozen snow bank.

I turned my nose into the . . . yipes . . . cold north wind and set a course that would take me directly to the snowbound car. I could hear the whine of the tires as she switched from Forward to Reverse in an attempt to rock the car out of the snow. It wasn't working, of course. I could have told her that. If she would just sit still and be patient, help was on the way.

Geothermal Energy. It's pretty impressive that a dog would know so much about heavy-duty scientific stuff, isn't it? You bet. A lot of your ordinary mutts would have just stood around saying, "Duhhhhhh," while the Lady of the House was trapped inside a snowbound car. Not me, fellers. On this outfit, any time we can apply science and mathematics to the daily problems of life, we do it.

It didn't take me long to reach the stranded vehicle. I marched up to the right rear tire and . . . SPLAT! She was still spinning her tires in the . . . SPLAT! You know, if she would just shut off the motor and sit still for a few . . . SPLAT!

On the other hand, if I skipped the rear tires and concentrated my efforts on the front tires, I would reduce the risk of getting plastered by flying snow, right? No problem there. I simply made a little detour, trotted around to the left side of the car, and marched up to the left front wheel. Pretty shrewd, huh?

I eased up to the tire and gave it a routine sniffing, checking it for scent. This wasn't really necessary but it's something we always do as a precautionary measure. Against what? We're not entirely clear about that, but the point is that dogs have always done it this way and that's what we do.

I finished the Snifferation in a matter of seconds, then went straight into the Geothermal Positioning Procedure. Here, a dog must position all four feet on the ground, so that the weight of his enormous body is equally distributed. Put too much weight on one side and it can throw the whole deal off kilter.

See, before we release the Geothermal Energy Fluid, we must be sure that the Launching Platform, so to speak, is perfectly level, square, plumb, and so forth. It's a lot of trouble, keeping things square and level, and a lot of mutts wouldn't go to the trouble, but with me it's a matter of routine.

It took a while but I got everything lined up, and then I was ready to move on to the next phase of the procedure. In this phase, we use huge hydraulic pumps that actually raise one of the legs of the Launching Platform. No kidding. In this case, it was the right rear leg of the . . .

HUH?

A woman was standing over me. She was wearing a heavy coat and a fur hat. Her nostrils were flared out like the head of a rattlesnake and her teeth were clenched like . . . gulp. I had seen this woman before . . . not so very long ago, in fact, and I had a feeling that it was . . .

"Get away from my car, you oaf! Haven't you done enough?"

Okay, it was Sally May. Did you think it was Monster Woman? So did I, just for second, but then I knew it must be Sally May. She had two kids, right? There were two children inside the car, and in fact, one of them (Little Alfred) was sticking his head out the window and . . . well, grinning about something.

Why was he grinning? Was I grinning? Heck no. I could see at a glance that Sally May was . . . well, in a pretty serious frame of mind, shall we say. Maybe she didn't understand that I had rushed back to melt the snow away from her . . .

You won't believe what she did. I was shocked to the bone. She snatched the hat off her head and *threw* it at me!

"Get away from here! Scat! Shoo!"

Gee whiz, I'd only been trying to . . . fine. If she wanted her car to stay in the snow bank for the rest of the day, if she didn't want my help, I could scat. But the next time she ran off the road and got herself stuck in a snow bank . . .

Sniff, sniff.

You know, that hat of hers had a pretty interesting smell. It reminded me a whole lot of . . . rabbits. Have we ever discussed Rabbits and Bunnies? We've got quite a number of bunnies on our ranch and I've made countless attempts to catch one, but with no success. They're clever little snots and experts at hiding in pipes and lumber piles.

But here was a nice little rabbit skin hat, lying in the snow. Heck, if she didn't want it . . .

"Put down my hat! Come back here, you . . . Hank, GIVE ME THAT HAT!"

Holy smokes, she was chasing me again!

Anyway, I didn't have the slightest interest in chewing on her ugly old hat anyway, so I, uh, dropped it and ran, one step ahead of . . . OOF! . . . a snowball that she launched in my direction. Actually, I was about half a step too slow and she nailed me right in the ribcage. Did it hurt? You bet it did. Don't ever let anyone tell you that Sally

May's a bad shot with a rock or a snowball. She can knock the eye out of a potato at twenty yards.

Beyond that range, she's not so great, but she connects often enough to be considered dangerous. My best advice is . . . don't ever give her a shot, she's liable to drill you.

Anyway, I was saddened by this latest turn of events, and I must admit that it made me wonder all over again . . . WHAT DOES A DOG HAVE TO DO TO PLEASE THESE PEOPLE?

You try to give 'em an escort off the ranch and they get mad. You try to free their cars from a snow bank and they get mad. You pick up an old hat they've thrown away and they get mad.

I don't know. It's very discouraging.

CHAPTER EIGHT

Pete Captures
the Deep Freeze

You probably think that Sally May's car remained stuck in the snow bank for the rest of the day and that she never made it to town, right?

Well, it could have turned out that way, and maybe even should have turned out that way, since she had screeched at me and rejected my offer of help. But she got lucky. Just as I was leaving the scene, guess whose pickup came down the road. Loper's.

He'd been feeding alfalfa hay to the cows on the north end of the ranch and he'd come back to load up some more hay. Sally May saw him coming and waved her arms for help. (Notice that she didn't screech hateful words or chunk snowballs at *him*.)

Loper drove up to the car and got out. Sally May

began talking and making bold gestures with her hands and arms. I couldn't hear every word of their conversation, but I did manage to pick up a few clues. Several times she jabbed a finger in my direction and when she raised her voice, I heard her say something about "that dog."

Do you see the meaning of this? She was blaming ME! Did it ever occur to her that the mastermind behind the whole incident was her precious kitty? Of course not. In her eyes, Pete could do no wrong and I could do no right. It made everything easy for her, don't you see. Any time something went wrong on the ranch, she never had to waste time looking for the villain. She always knew she could pin the blame on Old Hank.

Grumble, mutter. Oh well. I would settle my accounts with Mister Perfect Kitty. I wasn't sure yet what drastic course of action I would follow, but he would pay. You can fool Hank the Cowdog once in a row, and sometimes even twice or three times in a row, but sooner or later, the chickens will come home to root.

Rot. Roast.

Roost. The chickens will come home to the roost to rot.

The chickens will come home to ROOST. There we go.

I lingered and watched. Loper hooked a log chain onto the car and the pickup, put the pickup in four-wheel drive, and dragged the car back into the road. Sally May thanked him with smiles and happy words, and drove on to town.

There were no smiles or happy words for me, of course, but I can't spend my whole life brooding over all the injustice in the world or feeling sorry for myself. Yes, by George, I can!

It wasn't fair!

There, I've said it. My words have been entered into the Record Book of Life.

I marched away from the scene with my head held high. I had nothing to be ashamed of and my conscience had been cleared of all wrongdoing. I went in search of Kitty.

Near the front of the machine shed, I encountered Company B of the Security Division's Elite Guards—Drover. Do you think he was still lying in the snow, wounded and suffering with his bad leg? No sir. He was on all four feet and looked as healthy as a horse.

He greeted me with his usual silly grin. "Oh, hi. Did you get Sally May out of the snow?"

"Drover, it makes me suspicious when I return

from a dangerous mission and find that your leg has been miraculously healed."

"Yeah, it's much better now, and thanks for asking."

I narrowed my eyes at the runt. "I didn't ask but maybe I should have. How do you account for this dramatic improvement?"

"Well, you know the old saying."

I waited. "I probably do know the old saying, but maybe you could refresh my memory."

"Oh, okay. Let me think here." He wadded up his face in a display of great concentration. "You know, I can't remember, but it was a really neat old saying."

"Great. There's an old saying that explains how your leg healed itself and you can't remember it? Think harder, I want to hear this."

"Okay, let me think here." He squinted one eye and rolled the other one around. "Wait, I think I've got it: 'The hills of time are wounded.'"

I ran that back and forth through my mind. "That doesn't make sense. Think harder."

"Well, okay." He squinted and grunted and probed the thimble of his mind. "Here we go: 'The wounded heels of time are . . . blistered.'"

My eyeballs rolled up inside my head. "Drover, is it possible that you're trying to say, 'Time heals all wounds'?"

His face bloomed into a smile and he began hopping up and down. "That's it! How'd you know?"

"I know because I know all wise old sayings. Here's another one for you: 'He who fakes a wounded leg will get a knot upon his head.'"

"I never heard that one."

"I just made it up and I suggest you start thinking about it."

His gaze drifted up to the clouds. "He who fakes a wounded leg . . . will get a knot upon his head. You know, it doesn't quite rhyme, does it?"

I stuck my nose in his face and gave him a snarl. "Forget rhymes. Forget your counterfeit leg. Where's the cat?"

"The cat?"

"Yes, the cat. You remember cats? Meow? Hiss? Purr?"

"Oh yeah . . . cats. You know, we've got one here on the ranch. Old Pete."

"Right. And where is he? I'm fixing to make hamburger out of Old Pete."

"Boy, I love hamburger."

"WHERE IS HE?!"

Drover shrank back and gave me a wounded look. "Gosh, you don't need to scream."

"I'M NOT SCREAMING!" I screamed. "For the last time, where is the hamburger?"

"Well . . . I think Sally May keeps it in the deep freeze."

"Thanks. That's all I need to know." I whirled away from the little dunce and began marching toward the . . . I whirled around and marched back. "Did you say that Pete is hiding in the deep freeze?"

"No, the hamburger."

"Pete is hiding hamburger in the deep freeze?"

"No, Pete's hiding . . . Sally May keeps . . ." Suddenly he burst into tears and collapsed on the ground. "I don't know what I was saying! I'm so confused! I can't think when you scream at me!"

I gave him time to sniffle his way through this latest crisis. "All right, son, I'm no longer screaming. I'm speaking to you in a calm tone of vone. We can discuss this like grown, mature dogs."

He peeked out from behind his front paws. "What's a vone?"

"It's an electrical device that transmits a human voice from one place to another. Are you saying the cat has been using the phone?"

"Well . . ."

"Because if he has . . ." I began pacing, as I often do when . . . we've already discussed that. "Okay, let's go back to the beginning. According to your testimony, Pete has been hiding in the deep freeze and he's making secret calls on Sally May's phone.

This is very important information, Drover, and it throws the case in a whole new direction." Drover let out a groan. "Please don't groan in the middle of my interrogation."

"Help!"

"Your information has raised two crucial questions, Drover. How did Pete get into the deep freeze, and to who or whom was he speaking on the phone? If we can come up with answers to those two questions . . ." I noticed that Drover was staring down at the ground, shaking his head, and muttering under his breath. "Now what's wrong?"

"This is crazy. I don't know what we're talking about. I never said any of that stuff."

"You didn't say that Pete has been . . ."

Suddenly it occurred to me that this whole conversation about the cat was . . . well, pretty ridiculous. Think about it. A cat living in a deep freeze? And talking on the telephone? It made no sense at all. Yet somehow . . .

I eased my way over to Drover's side. "Drover, we need to have a little talk. I feel that we've been having trouble communicating. Have you noticed that?"

He bobbed his head up and down. "Yeah, and it's starting to worry me. I hope we're not the cause of it."

"We? You mean, you and I?"

"Yeah. If we're the cause of it, then maybe something's wrong with us."

"Explain that."

"Well, I'd hate to think that we're just a couple of . . . dumb dogs."

"Dumb dogs?" Those words sent a jolt all the way out to the end of my tail. I paced a few steps away from him. "Well, I . . . I must say this takes my breath away, Drover. To be honest, I'd never even considered such a possibility."

"Yeah, me neither, but now I'm beginning to wonder."

There was a long moment of silence, as each of us grippled with this grappling dilemma. Was it possible . . . could it be . . . ? My gaze drifted around ranch headquarters and came to rest on Pete. He was perched on top of the gatepost. He seemed to be watching us and listening. He smirked and waved a paw at me.

A thought began to take shape in the back of my mind.

"Wait, hold everything. I'm beginning to see light at the end of the turnip. It's not us, Drover. It's Pete!" I marched over to Drover's side. "Don't you get it? He's the cause of this!"

"He is?"

"Yes, of course." I began pacing again. "How could I have been so blind? He's been setting us up, Drover, using us, manipulating us, putting us into awkward situations that cause us to babble and talk nonsense."

"You mean . . ."

"Yes. He's been using cattish schemes and dirty tricks. First the phony Escort Service and now this crazy story about him living in the deep freeze and talking on the phone. Where do you suppose it's all been coming from?"

"Well, I think you . . ."

"It came from Pete. He planted that story about the deep freeze, hoping it would throw us off balance. And you know what? It almost worked." I whirled around. "But we exposed him just in time, and now we're ready to strike back. I've had it up to here, Drover."

"You have?"

"Yes. Here, listen to this song."

Right there, before his very ears, I performed a song.

I've Had It Up To Here

I really don't enjoy this stuff.
I think I've had about enough
Of Mister Kitty Cheater's brand of fun.

The little scrounge plays dirty tricks,
I fall for them like a ton of bricks.
Old Pete must think that I am really dumb.

  I'm here to tell you that I'm not,
  Although my life has gone to pot.
  The kitty has enjoyed a string of luck,
      that's all.
  How hard is it to fool a dog
  Who's trusting almost to a flaw?
  An honest dog is just a sitting duck.

That deal he hatched with Sally May,
I fell for it, to my dismay.
She screeched at me and drove into the ditch.
I've tried and tried to win her heart,
Events keep pushing us apart.
And Sally May has changed into a witch.

  I'm sure she didn't really know
  That I was worried 'bout the snow.
  I mean, that icy road was slippery.
  I was scared to death she'd have a wreck.
  Sure 'nuff, she did, then what the heck . . .
  She tried to make a wreck out of me!

There's something very much amiss
When I get blamed for stuff like this.
It's very hard for me to understand

How a sneaking, sniveling little wretch
Keeps having such a great success,
When I'm supposed to have the upper hand.

> I've had my fill of Kitty Cat,
> I wish I had a baseball bat.
> The time for my revenge is drawing near.
> My anger's very near the peak,
> There is no peace with such a sneak.
> And now I've finally had it up to here.
> I've had it up to here!

Pretty awesome song, huh? You bet. And don't forget that I wrote it on the spot.

I turned to Drover and gave him a triumphant smile. "The little sneak is trying to provoke us into open warfare, so guess what we're going to do next."

"Beat him up?"

"No. That would be stepping right into his trap. That's just what he wants, Drover. No, we're going to launch a counteroffensive that will blow his socks off. We're going to . . . *be nice*."

CHAPTER NINE

Our Clever Plan
to Defeat the Cat

Drover stared at me in amazement. "Be nice? You mean, to Pete?"

"Yes, to Pete, to Sally May, to everyone, Drover. We're going to change our behavior, become perfect dogs. We're going to fight fire with Pete's own medicine. I guarantee that it'll drive him nuts. Heh heh."

Drover gave his head a bewildered shake. "Boy, I sure get confused."

I patted him on the back. "It'll work, son. Just watch me and study your lessons. Now," I shot a glance at the cat, "we're fixing to put our plan into action. Let's move out."

We made our way up the gravel drive and to the yard gate. There sat Pete, perched on the top of the gatepost, with his tail wrapped around his haunches. He was wearing that insolent smirk of his, and it grew wider as we drew closer.

"Mmmmmm. My goodness, I think the cops are here."

"Yes, we were in the neighborhood and thought we'd drop by to say hello. Hello, Pete. By golly, how's your day going?"

"Well, Hankie, my day's been just swell. How about..." He leaned forward and smirked. "...yours. Tee hee. I guess you got in trouble with Sally May, hmmmm?"

Before I knew it, my ears jumped and my lips tried to twitch themselves into a snarl, but I managed to shut them down just in time. "Ha ha. Yes, old pal, you pulled a good one there. I mean, that business of escorting her car down the road...ha ha...that was one of your better tricks, Pete."

His eyes brightened. "It was pretty devilish, wasn't it?"

"It was really a nasty trick, and you know, Pete, I fell for it like a tub of bricks."

"You really did. I was afraid you might figure it out, Hankie."

"Nope, not me. Ha ha. You were miles ahead of me on that one."

He batted his eyes and began licking his paw.

"And now you're all worked up and aching for revenge, but, darn the luck, I'm sitting up here out of reach."

Drover and I exchanged winks. "No hard feelings, Pete. In fact, we came over here to offer our congratulations. Right, Drover?"

"Oh yeah. Right. You bet."

Get this. Old Pete's smirk dropped like a dead bird falling out of a tree. He stared at us with an open mouth. "I don't get it, Hankie. What's the catch?"

"No catch, Pete. We've said our congratulations, now we'll be on our way."

I gave Drover eye signals and we started walking away. Behind us, Pete said, "You're not going to try to chew down the gatepost?"

"Not this time, but thanks for the idea."

We kept walking. In the back of my mind, I could see Pete's face—his mouth hanging open, his eyes bugged out, his paw poised in midair, waiting to be licked. Then I heard his voice. "What would you think if I . . . came down, Hankie?"

"Suit yourself. We've got things to do. See you around."

We kept walking. There was a moment of silence, then we heard Pete's claws scratching on the post and his voice called out, "Hankie? I'm on the ground now. What do you think of that, hmmmm?"

Drover and I exchanged winks and giggles, and I yelled, "This snow's pretty cold, isn't it? I hope it doesn't aggravate that cough of yours."

We kept walking. Behind us, I heard the swish of paws in the snow, and a moment later Pete fell in step beside us. He beamed me a sour look. "Hankie, what are you trying to pull?"

"Pull? I don't know what you mean." I turned to Drover. "Do you know what he means?"

Drover's eyes came into focus. "Oh, hi. Did you say something?"

"Pete thinks we're trying to pull something. Do you know what he's talking about?"

"Oh, sure. He means . . ."

"Shhh!" I silenced him with a glare and turned to the cat. "Sorry, Pete, we have no idea what you're talking about."

"It won't work, Hankie."

"It? What is 'It'?"

"You're trying to be clever, but that goes against nature."

"Whatever you think, Pete. Now, if you'll excuse us, we've got some work to do."

Kitty stopped and we continued walking away at a leisurely pace. I heard Pete's voice behind me. "It'll never work, Hankie. You'll see."

Moments later, I peeked back over my shoulder and caught a glimpse of Kitty-Kitty, standing alone in the snow, twitching the last inch of his tail back and forth and glaring at us. Ha ha, hee hee, ho ho. Fellers, that was one confused cat!

I shot a glance at Drover. "What do you think, pal? Did we mess up his mind or what?"

"Yeah, tee hee, I've never seen him so shook up, tee hee."

"Just wait until Sally May comes back from town. Old Pete's really going to get ripped when he sees our next move."

"Gosh, what are we going to do?"

"Heh heh. Drover, we're going to spend the rest of the afternoon working on manners and polishing our Good Behavior Techniques."

He stopped in his tracks and stared at me. "Manners! Oh my gosh! That's pretty radical."

"Whatever works, Drover, whatever works. Heh heh."

Pretty amazing, huh? You bet. The mind of a dog is an awesome thing. Once aroused, it doesn't rest or leave a single stern untoned. Pete had started this war and we were going to finish it— even if that meant learning a few manners.

And that's exactly what we did for the rest of

the day. We held a crash course in Eating Techniques: slurpless chewing, dainty nibbling, no grabbing, no gulping or throwing up from eating too fast (that turns off Sally May, you know, when we dogs gobble food, and then throw up in front of her). We studied Patience and Prudence, Sitting Still, and other techniques I'd never tried before.

It was quite an afternoon and after several hours of it, we were worn to a frazzle. I had never dreamed that being a good dog could be such a pain in the neck. But we stayed with it. We studied and practiced, practiced and studied. By sundown, we were tired but ready. And that's when we heard Sally May's car coming down the road, its tires crunching ice and frozen snow.

I shot a glance at Drover. "Okay, son, Battle Stations! Follow me."

We went streaking northward toward the county road, making our way across ice and snow and frozen tundra. As we roared past the yard gate, I caught a glimpse of Kitty. He was wearing a gleeful smile and called out, "Oh goodie, you're going to escort her back to the house. What a smashing idea, Hankie. Don't forget: stay in front and go slow."

"Got it, pal. Thanks a bunch."

Heh heh. Little did he know.

We arrived at the mailbox just as Sally May

was turning off the county road, onto the private road that led to the house. Through the window glass, I could see her eyes coming at me like bullets. Her lips moved, forming words I couldn't hear. No doubt she thought I was going to position myself in the middle of the road and lead her down to the house, and she was getting herself worked up to screech at me again.

Heh heh. I had prepared a little surprise for Sally May. Instead of trotting in front of her car (and repeating the same mistake that had gotten me in so much trouble), I took up the Lateral Escort Position beside the car and gave the order to launch the Welcome Home program.

Have we discussed Welcome Home? It's a dynamite program. Usually we save it back for occasions when Our People have been gone for several days, but I figured this would be a good time to put it into action. We needed something special, right? This was special.

Your well-executed Welcome Home consists of several stages that are pretty complicated and hard to pull off. Do we have time to go into all the details? Sure, why not.

In the first stage, the dog trots along beside the car in the Lateral Escort Position, which we've already discussed. In stage two, the dog begins barking, but these are not ordinary barks. They're called Joyful Barks. To do 'em properly, you have to get exactly the right pitch and ration the supply of air to the barking mechanism.

Then, in stage three, the show really gets exciting, as we go into Leaps and Spins. And get this. When Welcome Home is done right, we're doing all three stages at the same time! Pretty amazing, huh? You bet. It's a tough program to do even on dry ground and in good weather, but it's even more difficult when . . .

PLOP!

Watch out for that hole.

It's even more difficult when the ground is covered with snow, concealing pits and holes, rocks and trees and other objects that can . . .

PLOP!

. . . interrupt the celebration process and cause a dog to . . . well, take a spill and stick his nose into a snowdrift. Yes, it's a toughie, and most of your ordinary dogs wouldn't even attempt it with snow on the ground, but we not only attempted it, we DID it. With the exception of a couple of dives into the snow, it was a perfect presentation of Welcome Home.

We escorted the car around the front of the house, down the hill, and then around to the back of the house, all the way to the yard gate. Pete was still sitting beside the gate. He had watched the entire presentation and was wearing a frozen smirk.

"My, my, Hankie, this is something new."

"That's right, pal, and we're not finished yet." I turned to my assistant. "All right, Drover, let's form a line and go into Controlled Sit."

I know this is getting pretty complicated, all these new terms and technical information, but we really need to say a word or two about the Controlled Sit. In some ways, it's even more difficult than Welcome Home. It requires huge amounts of discipline and training.

What makes it so tough is that it comes right after Joyful Barks and Leaps and Spins, procedures that involve the outward display of exuberant emotions. Controlled Sit is the very opposite. It requires a dog to go from wild displays of joy into a very disciplined sitting situation, in which he must keep a tight rein on his emotions and sit almost motionless.

To be honest, I wasn't sure we could pull it off. I mean, we had practiced it all afternoon, but still . . . see, if you're a loyal dog, your heart is filled with joy when Your People return home, and the natural way of expressing it is to jump up on Your People and give them Juicy Licks on the face—or sometimes on the ankles, if a face isn't available.

But I felt in my heart that this was the wrong approach for Sally May. See, I knew from bitter experience that she didn't appreciate being greeted with Leaps and Licks. Why? I have no idea. It was one of the great unsolved mysteries of my life. I mean, you'd think . . .

She was a little strange and we needn't say any more about it. The point is, I knew she would be deeply impressed if we could pull off a Controlled Sit.

I turned to Drover. "Okay, son, sit tight and control yourself. She's fixing to get out of the car. No matter what happens, remain in the sitting position."

"Oh gosh, I hope I can do it."

"You can do it. We've trained for it. We've drilled and prepared. Now it's time for us to put all our training to the test. Discipline, Drover, discipline."

"Well, I'll try."

Sally May shut off the motor. She looked out the window and sat us sawing beside her door . . . saw us sitting, let us say, beside her so-forth. She narrowed her eyes and scowled. She muttered something under her breath. She opened the door and stepped out.

And all of a sudden . . .

CHAPTER TEN

Justice Strikes
the Cat

You think we broke under the strain, don't you? Go ahead and admit it. You think we were suddenly swept away on a tidal wave of emotional so-forth, broke discipline, and threw ourselves all over Sally May—much to the delight of Kitty-Kitty, who was lurking near the gate and watching the whole show.

Heh heh. Nope.

You'll be shocked and astounded to hear that we kept our formation and imposed discipline upon our feelings of love and devotion. I'm not saying it was easy. It wasn't. It was one of the toughest assignments of my whole career. I mean, we were both quivering with emotion—trembling, shivering, shaking, twitching.

Drover's eyes crossed under the strain. My front paws moved up and down. Every muscle and nerve in my enormous body cried out for a blessed release, but somehow I managed to keep them under control.

We didn't jump or lick. We just sat there, beaming looks of devotion to the Lady of the House. Was she impressed? She was majorly impressed, Big Time impressed. She looked down at us for a long time, and slowly the ice in her face began to melt. Yes, right in front of my eyes, I saw the change.

At first she seemed too shocked to speak, but then she said, "My stars! This is something new."

She closed the door and walked around to the other side of the car to help the kids out. I shot a glance at Drover. "Okay, it's time for Loyal Dogs Following. Let's go!"

In a flash, we leaped to our feet, fell in step behind Sally May, and followed her around to the other side of the car. While she was opening the door, we plopped ourselves down in the snow and went into another Controlled Sit.

Little Alfred stepped out of the car and saw us. "Hi, doggies. Did you miss us?"

Oh yes! In fact, I came within a whisker of breaking discipline and throwing myself into his arms. We were the best of pals, the boy and I, and my whole body ached to give him a proper home-coming. But, somehow, I resisted and stayed in formation.

Sally May gathered up Baby Molly in her arms, closed the car door, and moved toward the gate. My eyes drifted down to a patch of bare ice right in front of her. It would be very slick. Did she see it? *Sally May, be careful, watch your step.* She was carrying the baby, see, and if she slipped on that ice . . .

It was as if it was happening in slow motion. I watched as her right foot came down on the patch of ice and began to slide forward. She leaned back-ward and tried to catch her balance, but her foot kept sliding. She was going to fall, I could see it coming. She and Baby Molly were going to take a hard spill on the frozen ground! And there was nothing anyone could . . .

Then it came to me in a flash. It wouldn't be fun, but I knew what I had to do. I would have to offer up my body as a Safety Cushion! I leaped to my feet and threw myself into the path of her plunge to the ground. I got there without a second to spare. Sally May's feet went out from under her and she sat down hard on my . . . OOF . . . mid-section. Baby Molly started to cry as they landed with a thump. Sally May had given me a pretty

severe smashing, but both she and Baby Molly
came out of it with no broken bones or damage.

Little Alfred helped her to her feet and she
looked down at me with astonished eyes. "Do you
suppose he did that *on purpose*?"

"I think so, Mom. He's a pwetty good dog."

I coughed and staggered to my feet, trying to
catch my breath. Sally May blinked her eyes and

shook her head, then her lips turned up in a smile. "Well, I never . . . Hank, I don't know if you meant to do that or not, but I could have broken my neck, or dropped the baby, or . . . I don't even want to think about it. I believe you deserve a reward. Alfred, honey, bring Hank a couple of strips of bacon." She bent down and patted me on the head. "Thank you."

Did you hear that? Wow! She had thanked me, and I was fixing to receive the Coveted Bacon Award! Could it get any better than that? Yes, it got even better. As Sally May crept across the ice and through the gate, guess who tried to butt into my deal and get some undeserved attention.

Mister Lurk and Smirk. Pete.

See, it had just about killed his soul that I had won some points with Sally May, and he just couldn't stand it. He shot me a hateful glare and started following Sally May toward the house, rubbing her ankles and purring. Tee hee. Maybe you can guess what happened. Pete got himself tangled up in her feet and she stepped on his tail.

His eyes bulged out and he cut loose with a loud, "*Reeeeeeeer!*"

Sally May tripped over him and said, "Sorry, Pete, but get out of the way."

Little Alfred was following behind his mother. "Get out of the way, Pete! You twipped my mom."

This was almost too delicious, and I came within a whisker of breaking discipline and going into a fit of wild, righteous laughter. But at the last second, I was able to impose Laughter Clamps and maintained a solemn face.

The cat picked himself out of the snow and shook all four paws, one at a time. His ears were pinned down on his head and he beamed me a glare. "Well, I guess you enjoyed that, Hankie."

"Me? Not at all, Pete. In fact, I'm sitting here sharing your pain and wishing there were something I could do to help you in this time of trouble."

Behind me, I heard Drover snort a muffled laugh. I struggled to keep a straight face—nay, a mournful face, one that expressed my deep sorrow that Pete had . . . tee hee . . . gotten exactly what he deserved, the pest. It was tough, but I got 'er done. I not only didn't laugh at Pete's misfortune, I didn't even smile.

I could see that this was killing him. My campaign to win the heart of Sally May was working to perfection, and Kitty had no idea what to do about it.

He came slithering through the snow, and by now the pupils of his eyes had widened. That's what cats do when they're mad, you know. The dark part of their eye gets big, revealing thoughts that are just as dark as their eyes. Oh, and his ears were still pinned down on his head.

"I know what you're doing, Hankie, but it won't work."

"I don't know what you mean, Pete. Are you suggesting . . ."

"You'll find out."

I didn't have time to wonder what that might mean. The back door opened and out came Little Alfred. And, holy smokes, even at a distance, I could see that he was carrying two strips of raw bacon draped over his left index finger. Drover and I exchanged looks of anticipation. We both began to quiver with excitement.

Drover said, "I don't know if I can sit still for this. I can already smell that bacon. Can I have a piece?"

"Are you nuts? I earned that by . . . okay, what the heck, I'll share."

"Gosh, thanks. Boy, I love bacon."

"Me too, but hold your position. Remember: manners and discipline."

Drover clamped his jaws together and put on a brave face. "Okay, I'll try."

"That's the spirit."

We watched as Little Alfred approached us on the snow-covered sidewalk. Pete was also watching, and as the lad walked up to the gate, Pete struck like a jungle tiger. He dived through the air and snatched our bacon strips out of Alfred's hand, and scampered away.

There we sat, Drover and I, waiting for the awards ceremony to begin, and suddenly the party was over. Nothing remained of our hopes and dreams but Kitty's tracks in the snow and the lingering aroma of luscious, yummy bacon.

I was too stunned to speak. Drover broke into tears. "He stole our bacon! Pete stole our reward for being good dogs! I wanted that bacon so bad, I can't stand it!" Through his tears, he stared at me. "Aren't you going to do anything?"

My mind was reeling. One voice inside my head screamed for revenge, but another voice was urging calm and restraint. "Stay calm, Drover. Let's try to work within the system."

"The system!" he squawled. "Systems don't work on cats because they cheat!"

"I know, I know, but let's hold our formation and see what happens."

Little Alfred's face had turned a deep shade of red and he beamed a hot glare toward the iris patch, where the thief had taken refuge. We could hear him smacking and slobbering as he devoured our Bacon Award.

Pete, that is, not Little Alfred. Pete was smacking and so-forthing.

Little Alfred raised a fist and shook it at the cat. "I'm going to tell my mom!" And with that threat hanging in the crisp air, the boy stomped back into the house. Moments later, we heard his voice. "Mom, Pete stole the bacon from my doggies!"

I shot a glance at Drover. "You see? The wheels of justice are beginning to turn."

"Well, I hope they run over Pete's tail, the mean old thing. My heart's just broken!"

"I understand, son, but try to be brave. Hold the formation and maintain Iron Discipline. This could get very interesting."

We waited. I kept one eye on the iris patch and the other on the back door. Pete's face poked around the side of the house. He was licking his lips and . . . you probably guessed . . . smirking.

He saw us and waved a paw. "The bacon was delicious, Hankie. I hope you didn't mind sharing it. You're such a nice doggie."

I wasn't sure I could hold myself back. My vision went red. I could feel pressure behind my eyes. I could hear thunder rumbling deep inside the volcano of my . . . something. My heart, I suppose. I could hear the rumbling of molten lava and the hissing of steam.

And then, beside me, Drover said, "Git 'im, Hankie, beat 'im up!"

I almost lost control and surrendered myself to the savage instincts that were urging me to make salad out of the scheming little cat, but just then the back door burst open.

You may not know this, but we dogs have learned to read Sally May's mood by the sound of the screen door opening. When it merely opens and closes, she's in a good mood. When it flies open and hits the side of the house with a loud crack, we know it's time to lay low and take cover.

The screen door opened with a loud crack. It sent a shiver down my backbone, and I had to struggle to keep from highballing it down to the calf shed—the place where on more than one occasion I had sought refuge from Sally May's . . . uh . . . sharp tongue and broom.

Remember that song about Sally May? "When she's angry, when she's wrathful, the trees run for cover. And when she speaks of her displeasure, the mountains hide their faces."

No kidding, it's true. Hey, when Sally May's on the peck, all life on the ranch comes to a standstill.

She came boiling out of the house. Her face showed all the signs of danger: flaming eyes, flared nostrils, lips as thin as nails. Just the sight of her turned me into a melting blob of dog hair.

Drover let out a gasp. "Oh my gosh, we'd better run!"

"Hold your ground, son. Let's see what happens."

"Yeah, but..."

"Shhhh. Listen."

Her eyes darted around the yard. She saw us sitting beside the gate—two faithful dogs who had been robbed and cheated. Little Alfred joined her.

"Where is the cat?" she asked. The boy pointed toward the iris patch. She started toward the northwest corner of the house. "Pete? Kitty? Here, Kitty."

I couldn't believe this next part. Any dog in his right mind would have quit the country when he heard the crack of the screen door, but Pete . . . see, he'd had very little experience with the Thermonuclear side of Sally May's personality. Oh, and he was also an incredible dumbbell.

You know what he did? He came sliding out of the iris patch, purring and rubbing against the side of the house. Then he went over to Sally May and started wrapping himself around her ankles. He had no idea what was fixing to fall on top of his head. But I did. Tee hee.

I loved it!

She reached down and snatched him off the ground. I mean, she didn't just pick him up, she *snatched* him up so fast, it actually caused his smirk to evaporate. Maybe he had begun to realize that, this time, something was different.

Sally May held him up to her face. "You're a naughty cat. You stole bacon from the dogs and you didn't deserve it. Shame on you!"

She pitched him out into the snow. He pinned down his ears, fired an angry look at us dogs, and went scampering off to the north side of the house.

You talk about quivering with joy and excitement! I could hardly sit still. I wanted to do flips in the air and bark a rousing approval for a job well done, but, somehow, I maintained Iron Discipline and held the formation. So did Drover. I was proud of the little mutt.

CHAPTER ELEVEN

I Win the Heart of Sally May at Last!

On the porch, Little Alfred let out a yell. "Way to go, Mom!"

She walked back to the porch. Her shoulders sagged and her eyes seemed troubled. "I hate getting mad, I just hate it, but what can a woman do? I discipline the dogs when they're bad, and it's only fair that I do the same to the cat." Her lip began to tremble. "But sometimes I think I'm turning into . . . a wicked witch. Just look at me!"

And then, before our very eyes and ears, she sang a song. No kidding. Here's how it went.

What Is a Woman to Do?

This morning I thought that our Hank was
    a villain.

112

I screamed at him, chased him, and wanted
    to kill him.
I hefted a snowball and managed to drill him.
But what is a woman to do?

I've hinted to Loper to tie him up tight.
The beast, after all, isn't overly bright.
But tying up dogs just doesn't seem right.
So what is a woman to do?

> My needs are so small, just order,
>   that's all.
> The same as you'd find in a school.
> If I dared relax and ignored these attacks,
> The powers of darkness would rule.

And look at me now, I scolded the cat!
My anger spilled out like a boiling vat.
I know it's my job, but I feel like a rat.
But what is a woman to do?

They test me and try me, they've made
    me a cop.
But if I don't do it, then where will it stop?
This ranch is my home, an asylum it's not.
So what is a woman to do?

> Am I losing my touch or asking too much?
> After all, I'm not running a zoo.

I'd rather not nag,
They all think I'm a hag,
But that's what a woman must do.

Pretty spooky song, huh? I thought so. I mean,
let's face it, she had mentioned my name, right? And
that made me nervous, even though I had changed
my ways and become a model of good behavior.

When she'd finished, Sally May beamed dark
glares around the yard, then let her gaze drift down
to her son. "And that goes for you too, young man.
This is my home and we'll follow my rules. If that
makes me the wicked witch, so be it."

The boy nodded. "Okay, Mom, but you're not a
wicked witch."

A smile tugged at the corners of her mouth and
her eyes softened. "Thank you, sweetie, but you're
probably the only one on this ranch who thinks so."

"Can I give the doggies their bacon now? They're
still waiting."

She blinked several times and turned her eyes
on . . . yipes . . . on us. I felt as though someone had
snapped on a powerful searchlight . . . or an X-ray
machine and pointed it right at my heart. Gulp. Did
I have any naughty thoughts swimming through
the dark waters of my soul? Because if I did, she
would see them.

She always saw naughty thoughts. There was no hiding from her. That gaze had a way of prowling through a dog's heart and mind, looking in every drawer, every closet, every cookie jar, until she found a naughty thought.

I felt myself shrinking and melting under the glare of her X-ray vision. My head sank. One eye began to twitch. Suddenly, I was seized by a powerful urge to . . . well, bite myself on the tail, if you can believe that. Why? I don't know. She just does that to me . . . those eyes . . .

But then . . . she smiled! Whew! I dared to tap out a slow rhythm with my tail. Then she said, "They've earned their bacon, and I'll give it to them myself."

She went into the house. I almost fainted with relief. So far, so good. Moments later she returned, this time opening the screen door without throwing it back against the side of the house. This was looking better and better. She came down the sidewalk, holding two strips of raw bacon on a paper towel.

I felt a surge of Bacon Lust roaring through my body. Would I be able to contain myself and hold back my savage instincts? I wasn't sure I could. This was new territory for me—eating raw bacon with manners.

She came through the yard gate and stood in front of us. A peculiar smile rippled across her lips as she looked into my eyes. "Hank, I don't know what's come over you. This is quite a switch for us, isn't it? Why, this very morning I wanted to . . ." She didn't finish the sentence.

Uh . . . yes ma'am. It was quite a switch.

"Well, I'm proud of you for learning some manners. And for not beating up the cat, even though he probably deserved it. You've been a good dog, Hank, and here is your reward."

Did you hear that? *Sally May called me a good dog!* WOWEEE!

Maybe you think I was overpowered by Bacon Lust, snatched the bacon out of her fingers, wolfed it down, and ruined everything. No sir. I had come this far and I had no intention of messing things up. And, hey, I even let Drover have the second piece of bacon.

With a tongue that was as soft as rabbit fur . . . oops, let's change that. With a tongue as soft as velvet, I coaxed the strip of bacon from her outstretched fingers. I saw her eyebrows rise. She was impressed. Gently and tenderly, I eased the bacon out of her fingers, brushed it into my mouth, and . . . you won't believe this part . . . chewed it twenty-three times.

Yes sir, twenty-five times. No gulping, no gagging on half-chewed bacon, no throwing up in front of the Lady of the House. After chewing it twenty-seven times, only then did I pull the Flush Lever and send it sliding down the pipes to my awaiting stomach.

Pretty amazing, huh? You bet. Drover did pretty well too, although his eating wasn't quite as refined as mine. But the important thing is that Sally May was overwhelmed. After years and years of trying, I had finally managed to win her approval!

She gave each of us a rub on the head. But then . . . oops . . . she smelled her hand and made a face. I held my breath and waited for the hammer to fall. But she smiled and said, "Well, every journey begins with the first step," and went back into the house.

Whew! The awards ceremony was over and it had been a huge success. Okay, she had made one little reference to Dog Odor, but she had left the ceremony wearing a smell.

A smile, that is. She had left wearing a smile.

I turned to Drover. "Congratulations, son. This may be the Security Divison's finest hour. We've not only won back the heart of Sally May, but we've delivered the cat a crushing defeat."

Drover was as excited as I was. "Yeah, hee hee, Sally May called him a naughty cat. I never thought I'd hear that."

"It was delicious, wasn't it? I only wish we had it on film, so that we could watch it over and over— Pete getting the scolding he has deserved for years! Ho ho, hee hee, ha ha! And speaking of Mister Kitty Moocher . . ."

I swept my gaze across the yard, expecting to see

Pete sulking and glaring daggers at us. Hmmm. He was nowhere in sight. I pushed myself up and trotted around the north side of the fence, where I had a clear view of the iris patch.

Drover followed me. "Gosh, he's gone. I wonder where he went."

"Oh, he's probably off pouting. You know cats. They can't take a telling, they refuse to accept punishment or any kind of discipline. But do we care?"

"Well . . ."

"No, we don't care, Drover. What matters is that we delivered him a smashing defeat, and now we can go back to the office and bask in the glory of our triumph. This is a great day for the ranch!"

Proud and victorious, we formed a column and marched down to the Security Division's Vast Office Complex. There, we scratched up our gunnysacks, did the usual Three Tunes Return . . . Three Turns Routine, let us say, and collapsed.

Could two dogs ask for more? No sir. This was the very best that life had to offer: a warm gunnysack bed, success in battle, victory over an old enemy, Sally May's approval, and the Coveted Bacon Award.

WOW!

We spent the rest of the evening re-living the events of the day and . . . might as well say it . . .

gloating. Yes, we indulged ourselves in two solid hours of shameless gloating. I doubt that history could provide an example of two dogs who gloated more or enjoyed it more than we did.

It was absolutely delicious—two hours of non-stop gloating and bragging, without one shred of guilt or shame. We giggled and snickered, guffawed and snorted, slapped each other on the back, and roasted Pete's name over the fires of . . . something. The fires of our happiness, I suppose, although that doesn't sound exactly right, "fires of happiness."

The fires of our devilish delight. That's better.

Anyway, we spent the rest of the evening in wild celebration and by sundown, we were both exhausted. I had never realized that gloating could be so tiring. Spent and exhausted, we found ourselves staring into each other's eyes. A deep silence moved over us.

Drover broke the silence. "Well . . . what do we do now?"

"I'm not sure. I guess we've celebrated as much as we can celebrate."

"Gosh, I hate to quit. I wish there was more."

"Yes, me too, but all good things must come to an end."

"How come?"

"Well . . . because they do, Drover. If good things

lasted forever . . ." Suddenly I had a thought. "Wait a second. Maybe there is a way we can stretch this out."

"Oh goodie! How?"

I rose to my feet. "Drover, we've spent the afternoon gloating to ourselves, but we've neglected the highest and most refined form of gloating. There's a whole new world of gloating we haven't experienced."

"There is?"

"*We haven't gloated in front of Pete!* See, we could be sharing the joy of our victory with Pete . . . and making him miserable!"

Drover grinned. "Gosh, I never thought of that. Hee hee. That would be even better, wouldn't it?"

"Indeed it would. It would be gloating multiplied by gloating, gloating squared. I don't know why we didn't think of this sooner."

"Well, we tried but he was gone."

"Good point. Well, he'll be back at the iris patch by now. Come on, son, let's go find the little sneak."

We left the office and went streaking down to the yard gate. There, I called his name. "Pete? Kitty? Hey, Pete, report to the yard gate at once. We've got something we want to share with you." Drover and I exchanged winks and snickers. We waited. "Pete?" No answer. "Pete, this is the Head of Ranch Security speaking. I am ordering you to report to the gate!"

Nothing. Not a sound.

Drover and I exchanged puzzled glances. "Gosh, what do we do now?"

I plunked myself down in the snow. "We'll sit right here and wait. I mean, who does that cat think he is? He'll show up, and when he does, he'll hear plenty about this."

I knew the little pest would show up. He always did. But you know what?

Well, you'll find out. It was pretty shocking.

Our Final Triumph
Over the Cat

The minutes dragged by. The sun went down and the cold winter night settled around us. Bright stars twinkled in the . . . no, they didn't. No stars twinkled because the sky was cloudy.

We waited. And waited. An hour dragged by. I was dying of boredom and getting madder by the second. You know me: I hate to wait. And I especially hate waiting on a sniveling little cat.

Around seven o'clock, the back door opened and Sally May came out with the supper scraps. Drover and I were sitting beside the gate in our Perfect Dogs Position. Once again, Sally May was deeply impressed. She heaped praise upon us and gave us all the scraps: some outstanding trimmings of roast beef, two plops of mashed potatoes and gravy, and three pieces of homemade buttermilk biscuit.

No question about it, this was a fist feat for a king. And it was all ours. There was no Pete around to mooch, whine, argue, or fight.

Sally May wished us goodnight and went into the house. Drover sniffed the scraps. I sniffed the scraps. Our eyes met.

Drover's voice trembled. "Something's wrong. I'm not even hungry."

"I know, me neither."

"This is crazy. Those are the best scraps we've had in weeks."

"I know, and all we can do is stare at them." I paced a few steps away. "You know who's the cause of this, don't you? It's Pete. He has not only disrupted our Gloating Ceremony, but now he has ruined our supper."

"Gosh, maybe the coyotes ate him."

"The coyotes didn't eat him, Drover. Don't you get it? He's hiding from us. He's somewhere on this ranch, chickling and snuckering at all the damage he's caused."

"You mean . . ."

"Yes. This is another of his sneaky tricks. Well, he'll never get by with it. Come on, son, we're going to turn headquarters upside down until we find the little creep. And if we have to, we'll *drag* him back down here. Let's move out."

I knew where he was—in the machine shed. That's exactly the place where a cat would hide. We marched up the hill and burst into the machine shed.

"Okay, Pete, game's over. Come out with your tail up. It's time for you to get back to the yard." Nothing, not a sound. "Okay, buddy, you want us to tear the place apart? We'll tear the place apart."

He thought he could hide from us? Ha. Little did he know. We tore the place apart, looked in every corner, under every box and paint bucket and . . . well, you might say he wasn't there. And suddenly I realized just how serious this crisis had become.

Drover's lower lip began to tremble. "Oh my gosh, I just know the coyotes ate him."

"Trust me, Drover, the coyotes *didn't* eat him. I'm telling you, he's planned the whole thing to disrupt our lives. It's exactly the kind of nasty trick a cat would think of. No dog would ever stoop so low."

Drover glanced around with worried eyes. "What'll we do?"

"We'll find him, Drover. We have no choice. Don't you see what he's done? He has robbed our lives of all meaning and purpose! Without Pete, gloating is pointless. Without Pete, scraps are merely scraps. Do you want to go on living like that?"

He sniffled. "I don't think I could stand it."

"All right, then let's find him and put our lives back together."

We continued our search. We checked the tool shed, scrap pile, and the chicken house. The chicken house was fun. We woke up twenty-seven head of brainless chickens and left 'em in squawking disarray, but . . . no Pete.

Again, I tried calling. "Pete, this is the Security Division again. We've got units all over the place. Ranch headquarters is surrounded. There's no way out. Give yourself up before this deal gets out of hand."

Drover was getting more worried by the second and I was getting madder. If at first you don't succeed, raise your voice, right? I did that. I screamed and yelled, threatened and even foamed at the mouth.

Nothing. Not a sound.

Drover was almost in tears by this time. "This is awful. Maybe you ought to try calling in a nicer tone of voice."

I stared at the runt. "What? A nicer tone of . . .

Drover, that is the dumbest thing you've ever said. He's a sneak, he's a cheat, he's a crooked little cat. I will never . . ." I gave it some thought. "Okay, it might work. Anything to get our lives back. I'll try *nice*, Drover, but if you ever breathe a word of this to anyone . . ."

"My lips are sealed."

"They'd better be. I'm putting my whole career on the line for this."

Do I dare reveal this next part? It's going to be pretty shocking but . . . well, maybe you've already figured it out. Okay, here it comes.

I spent the next hour walking through ranch headquarters and calling the stupid cat . . . calling Pete, that is, in a . . . choke, gork, arg . . . in a friendly tone of voice.

There it is. I'm ashamed to admit it but it's the truth. And, coincidentally, it worked.

We had called our way down to the corrals and had wasted hours of precious time on this ridiculous mission. Finally, as we stood in front of the saddle shed, we heard a familiar whiney voice coming from inside the feed barn.

Moments later, the villain appeared. He slipped through the crack at the bottom of the feed barn door and came sliding toward us. Yes, it was Pete, all right. I recognized all the signs. He was creeping along with his tail stuck straight up in the air, purring, rubbing his way down the corral fence, and wearing that same smirk that drives me nuts.

"Well, my goodness, it's Hankie. What brings you out on a night like this?"

My leaps lipped into a snarl. "You know exactly what we're doing here, you little fraud. We've come to take you back to the yard, where you belong."

"But I don't want to go back to the yard, Hankie. Sally May scolded me and pitched me into the snow, and I'm never going back. Cats hold grudges, you know."

I swaggered over to him and stuck my nose in his face. "Look, pal, you're going back to the yard, whether you like it or . . ."

"Ah, ah, ah." He raised a paw in the air. "Don't push your luck, Hankie. If you take me back, I'll just leave again. Do you want to guard me twenty-four hours a day?"

"Are you kidding? I would die of boredom. One minute with you is like a week with a toothache."

"In that case," he began rubbing on my front legs, "we'd better talk deal."

I backed away from the little python. "Deal? Me, make a deal with a cat? Ha! Are you crazy?"

He batted his eyes and started walking away. "Very well. You give me no choice."

My mind was tumbling and churning. "Pete, I'm ordering you . . ." He kept walking. I, uh, followed him—but slowly, at my own pace. "Hold up. Okay, Pete, let's talk deal. What's on your mind?"

He stopped and looked up at me with his weird yellow eyes. "I don't like this Nice Doggie business. It's unnatural. It's unwholesome. And it causes problems."

I turned a sneer toward Drover. "Did you hear that? He doesn't like our Nice Doggie business. Ha ha!" Drover didn't laugh, so I whirled back to the cat. "Is this a joke? Look, Kitty, for the first time in history, I'm on good terms with Sally May."

"I know, Hankie, and I don't like that."

I turned to Drover. "This cat's insane. He's twisted. If he thinks we're going to . . ."

Drover said, "I think we'd better do it."

I was so shocked, I couldn't breathe. I motioned for Drover to join me in a High Level conference off to the side, where Kitty Eavesdrop couldn't hear us. "Drover, his terms are totally unreasonable."

"Yeah, but he's got us over a barrel. It's the only way we'll get our lives back."

"So . . . you think . . ."

Drover nodded.

I heaved a deep sigh. This was one of the most difficult decisions of my whole career. I paced back and forth for several minutes, while Pete licked his front paw and Drover fretted. At last, I reached a decision. I marched back to the cat.

"Okay, Pete, you seem to be holding the big cards."

He grinned and batted his eyes. "I thought you'd think so. No more Nice Doggie?"

"No more Nice Doggie. And you'll come back to the yard? Tonight?" Pete nodded. "Okay, you've got yourself a deal. Now, let's put this whole ugly episode behind us and get down to the yard gate. We've got some scraps we need to fight over."

The three of us started walking back to the house, with Pete between us. He glanced up at me and said, "You know, Hankie, I think this is the beginning of a beautiful friendship."

"Yeah? You make me sick. You make me ill."

"But you love it, don't you?"

"Shut up, cat."

Five minutes later, we were fighting over supper. The scraps were great and we dogs got more than our share, tee hee. Drover and I chased the cat up a tree and spent the next two hours gloating, taunting, and barking our hearts out . . . oops . . . until an inflamed Sally May came to the door, screeched at us to be quiet, and threatened to send Loper out with the shotgun.

Hey, it was the Good Old Days again. We'd gotten our lives back and . . .

Do you find this confusing? I do, and I think it's gone far enough.

Case Closed.

Something's wrong with that cat. He's twisted, and I mean REALLY TWISTED.

Have you read all
of Hank's adventures?

Join Hank the Cowdog's Security Force

Are you a big Hank the Cowdog fan? Then you'll want to join Hank's Security Force. Here is some of the neat stuff you will receive:

Welcome Package
- A Hank paperback of your choice
- A free Hank bookmark

Eight issues of *The Hank Times* newspaper
- Stories about Hank and his friends
- Lots of great games and puzzles
- Special previews of future books
- Fun contests

More Security Force Benefits
- Special discounts on Hank books and audiotapes
- An original Hank poster (19" x 25") absolutely free
- Unlimited access to Hank's Security Force website at www.hankthecowdog.com

Total value of the Welcome Package and *The Hank Times* is $23.95. However, your two-year membership is **only $8.95** plus $4.00 for shipping and handling.

☐ Yes, I want to join Hank's Security Force. Enclosed is $12.95 ($8.95 + $4.00 for shipping and handling) for my **two-year membership**. [Make check payable to Maverick Books.]

WHICH BOOK WOULD YOU LIKE TO RECEIVE IN YOUR WELCOME PACKAGE?
CHOOSE ANY BOOK IN THE SERIES. **(#** _____ **) (#** _____ **)**
                                     FIRST CHOICE   SECOND CHOICE

_____ **BOY or GIRL**
YOUR NAME   (CIRCLE ONE)

_____
MAILING ADDRESS

_____
CITY   STATE   ZIP

_____
TELEPHONE   BIRTH DATE
_____ Are you a ☐ Teacher or ☐ Librarian?
E-MAIL

Send check or money order for $12.95 to:

Hank's Security Force   **DO NOT SEND CASH.**
Maverick Books   **NO CREDIT CARDS ACCEPTED.**
P.O. Box 549   *Allow 4–6 weeks for delivery.*
Perryton, Texas 79070

The Hank the Cowdog Security Force, the Welcome Package, and The Hank Times *are the sole responsibility of Maverick Books. They are not organized, sponsored, or endorsed by Penguin Group (USA) Inc., Puffin Books, Viking Children's Books, or their subsidiaries or affiliates.*